DREADFUL DOZEN

DREADFUL DOZEN

K.M. BENNETT

For my magnificent husband, who inspired me to put this story collection together.

Contents

1

The Red Light

Hello, whoever you are.

My name is Danica Burakova. I'm a life systems engineer on the TALUS-IQ ship bound for the new colony on TALUS. Just like you, I awoke before I was supposed to, while everyone else was still in cryosleep.

If you're reading this, I am dead. But if you're reading this, *you* don't have to die. Before you write me off as a madwoman, read the logs and transcripts. Then, make up your mind.

***

Danica's Log, December 21, 2300. Midday.

His smiling face was the first thing I saw. I felt like I was dying when I emerged from my cryostasis pod, so I welcomed his stabilizing arms. He looked right into my eyes, and his gray irises gave me something to focus on besides my pain and nausea. There was a cold persistence in that gaze, and I was reminded of a bird I saw once with unblinking eyes like that. I don't remember what kind.

"Hey there, Sleeping Beauty. You're finally awake."

He looked to be in his mid-to-late thirties. Hair the color of sandpaper, skin pale with a bluish hue beneath: someone who hadn't seen the sun in years.

With his gaze aimed at the floor, away from my nakedness, he extended an arm to me with a towel draped across it. I gave the towel a blank stare, feeling unsure about what to do and embarrassed about my confusion.

"It's normal." He tapped the lid of the pod with his finger. There was a warning written there:

STOP! DO NOT EXIT YOUR POD UNASSISTED. TO AVOID INJURY, PLEASE WAIT AT LEAST 30 MINUTES BEFORE ATTEMPTING TO WALK. CONFUSION IS NORMAL. FULL MEMORY RETURNS WITHIN SIXTY MINUTES IN MOST CASES. IF IT DOES NOT, PLEASE SEE YOUR MEDICAL UNIT.

I exhaled and grabbed the towel, wrapping myself up tight.

He frowned. "Are you scared?"

My voice didn't yet work, so I nodded.

"Of me?" And the way he said it, with a goofy and disarming grin, lowered my defenses. He extended a hand to me. His movements were slowed to a comical degree as if I were a skittish animal. "Mac Fogarty."

I shook the hand, and a scratchy laugh came out of my throat. It hurt.

"I'm...Danica." I actually couldn't remember my name for a moment.

"It's a pleasure to meet you, Danica. Now, I'm sorry to be the one to tell you this, but it appears that your cryostasis pod has malfunctioned." His eyes slid to a small red light labeled *maintenance* on the front of my pod. The other pods all blinked green lights, creating a pale green trail that led down the shining floors to the lone red beacon of malfunction.

With my heart pounding in my ears, my intestines became a ripcord and my stomach the parachute. I felt lightheaded and ready to throw up.

"Now, now. No need to panic. I happen to be just the fellow you need at the moment. I'm in charge of maintenance." He pointed to a badge over his left breast. The words swam before my eyes when I tried to focus. I couldn't read. "I'm the one who stays awake while you all sleep in case anything like this happens."

"So you can fix it?" I rasped.

"If you're a good girl," he said with a tilt of his head.

My spine went rigid as he guided me down from the pod to the floor. Getting my slippery feet in a stable position took my full attention, but as soon as I landed on the floor, I aimed a startled look at him and pulled the towel tighter around my body.

"I'm just kidding!" He gave my shoulders a gentle shake. "Of course I can fix it."

Relief flooded my cold body, warming me a little. My eyes fell on the warm-looking piece of terrycloth draped over the back of the chair where he'd been sitting. "I'll let it slide if you hand me that robe." I tried to smile, but my lips were trembling and all I could manage was a tight grimace.

He held the robe open while I struggled to find the coordination to put my arms in the sleeves while covering myself with the towel. As I pulled an arm through, I accidentally brushed his face with my hand. His skin was smooth from a fresh shave. Something musky and earthy met my nostrils. Maybe a hint of juniper? He certainly smelled good for someone who spent all their time alone.

"How long will it take?" I said, feeling tears spring to my eyes. My future began to flash before my eyes. What if he couldn't fix it and I had to live my whole life out before the rest of the colony woke up? We were too far out in our journey now for any aid to reach me. "How broken is my pod, exactly?"

"Calm down, Danica. I haven't had time to make a full assessment yet, but I'll get to that as soon as we get you warmed up."

"Why was it just my pod?" The room began spinning around me. What if I never saw my family again because I lived out my lifespan before they awoke? "Why me?" My eyes leaked small rivers of tears.

"You're a jumpy one, aren't you? There's no need to panic. What are you, one of the folks from the Risk Assessment department?"

"Engineering," I said. My entire outlook and demeanor immediately brightened. "I'm an engineer! I forgot myself for a minute."

His face became grim. "Be careful. You can't always trust your thoughts rights after waking up. Some people get freezerburn syndrome."

I quirked an eyebrow. "Freezerburn syndrome? That sounds made up."

"There's a fancier medical term for it, but it's impossible to pronounce. Some brains just can't handle the defrosting. Everything comes out all scrambled. There are large gaps in memory, even false memories. Hold on a second," he rummaged around in a drawer and pulled out a small manual. "Here, you can read about it."

Fast Facts About FreezerBurn Syndrome. On the back, there was a list of symptoms to watch out for. Confusion. Memory loss. Anger. Violent outbursts. Suicidal ideation.

I was relieved to find I could read again but disturbed by the information.

"Thankfully," he was smiling again, "I'm here to help you. If you have any confusing thoughts that need a reality check, just ask. It can help to have someone stable to help you keep a handle on reality."

"Thanks," I said, but I doubted I'd be confiding in a complete stranger like that. A faint memory of our pre-cryo training flickered back into my mind. I remembered now. Freezerburn syndrome had been mentioned, but it was deemphasized as extremely rare. At least, that's what I thought I remembered. That was the thing about this condition—you could have false memories. Did I create this one just because of what Mac said about it?

I rubbed my temples, trying to shake off the feeling of unreality. "I know this might seem like an odd request for someone who's been unconscious for who knows how long, but I'm exhausted. Is there someplace I can lie down for a while?" I needed to be alone with my memories, false or not.

"Of course. Most people do need to sleep a little to recover after the thawing process. Your body goes through a lot. Let me help you to a room."

My thoughts wandered to strange places, distracted by meaningless details, such as the stiffness of Mac's blue shirt and collar. It looked ironed. Maybe starched. People who took great care with their appearance tended to be detail oriented. I wanted to believe this of Mac so that I could have faith that he would be able to fix my pod.

***

Danica's Log December 21, 2300. Night.

After my nap, Mac gave me a tour of the open quadrants of TALUS-IQ. Upon waking all together, we were supposed to receive group orientation, but in the current circumstances, Mac would have to explain everything. He was mildly entertaining for someone who had been in isolation for so long. I found myself laughing at his corny jokes several times during the day.

He showed me his favorite coffee machine in the kitchen next to the Thornton lounge. Of the twenty machines, nineteen make coffee that tastes like motor oil while his preferred one has a yellow sticker on it to help him remember which is the best of the identical machines.

After we had our coffee, he insisted on showing me the horticultural wing that he called the Solarium. I feigned interest as a kindness since he's been alone for so long, even though I couldn't care less about plants. I've always killed any houseplant I touched. In contrast, Mac has been all alone for a year with nothing else to do.

His most prized creation was a hybrid tea rose that he bred himself. On each petal, a burst of yellow color pooled in the center and poured out gradually into a black outer edge. Each dense bloom was sprinkled all over with white specks like stars.

"I call this hybrid *Celestial Dusk.*" He cut one slender stem and put the bloom in my hand. Mac's not bad-looking, and I'm not the kind of girl who usually gets roses. My nose is usually buried in wires or blueprints too often for me to notice anyone or vice versa. So, I wasn't exactly displeased with the gift.

But now that the rose is sitting in a glass of water in my room, its presence makes me feel uneasy. I think it's because I hope I'm back in cryostasis before it dies. I'm reminded of an old fairy tale I used to love as a little girl: the one where the enchanted rose's death is linked to doom.

Mac hasn't yet said how long the repair will take since he's still evaluating the machine. But I think my hopes of it being fixed today are no longer viable. Being an engineer myself, I offered to help him with the machine when I heard him swearing at it, but he shooed me away and insisted that he can only do this work alone. All I can do is wait.

***

Danica's Log, December 22, 2300. Morning.

Sleep here is strange. Disjointed. It doesn't help that there's no sun to keep track of the hour, but the other thing is my dreams. Take last night. Deep in the night, I opened my eyes and saw the outline of a man blocking the light from coming in from the hallway. I squeezed my eyes shut for a few moments. I'm familiar with sleep paralysis, having experienced it a few times as a child, mostly during times of stress. I've learned that the shadow men are harmless, if terrifying. When I opened my eyes, the outline was gone, and I drifted back down into sleep.

The clock in my room said it was 8:00 UTC, which I mentally translated to 4:00 a.m. EST, whatever significance that time held so far removed from Earth. Clocks were essentially meaningless here, but they did help with making sure people could do their jobs on schedule and giving some semblance of temporal structure in the void of space.

I wished to sleep, but the worry that my mind was succumbing to freezerburn kept me awake. I decided to wander a little.

***

CHAT LOG SESSION WITH Nonintellectual Answer Network for Crew Year version - 2300 (N.A.N.C.Y)

December 22, 2300.

N.A.N.C.Y: Identify verified. Welcome, Danica Burakova. Please note that this is not an artificial intelligence. We are an unintelligent chat system, built for query and response.

Danica: What is the maintenance code for pod 329?

N.A.N.C.Y: Your query returned zero results. Please try again.

Danica: Pod status 329.

N.A.N.C.Y: Pod 329: Status, hatch open. Functioning, optimal.

Danica: Ignorant machine.

N.A.N.C.Y: I am an unintelligent chat system. Version year 2300. Copyright--

Danica: Command: stop.

Danica: Show all diagnostic reports for pod machine 329.

N.A.N.C.Y: Retrieving reports. Please wait...

N.A.N.C.Y: Access denied. Security clearance is insufficient for user Danica Burakova. Please contact your security officer for assistance.

Danica: I'm literally an engineer for TALUS-IQ. Check my security clearance again. I have the highest level.

N.A.N.C.Y.: Please contact your security officer for assistance.

Danica: Pod 329 is MY pod. I should be able to get diagnostic data on my pod.

N.A.N.C.Y.: Please wait...

N.A.N.C.Y.: Thank you for waiting. Please contact your security--

Danica: N.A.N.C.Y., you're kind of a bitch.

N.A.N.C.Y.: You are...

N.A.N.C.Y.: ...so welcome for the help. Thank you for using N.A.N.C.Y., an unintelligent chat system. Goodbye.

***

Danica's Log, December 22, Midday

I spent the morning hours roaming the halls. I tried getting some answers out of N.A.N.C.Y., but the program was worse than useless. For the most part, my journey was a fruitless endeavor, for one exception. The inner airlock door has a log of recent exits and entrances that appears on a digital display. I was surprised to find that there had been an exit on January 1, 2300. And according to the display, whatever load had left the ship that day had weighed 200 pounds.

***

Danica's Log, December 23, Morning

Sleep paralysis again last night. Every time I see the shadow man's outline in the doorway, I squeeze my eyes shut and tell myself he'll be gone soon. I've never had this happen two nights in a row before.

In the morning, a banging on my door awoke me, and I opened it to see Mac's normally patient face pinched in frustration.

"Not cool." His arms were crossed over his chest and he shook his head at me. "What gives, Danica? I know you're going through a lot right now with the defrosting process, but this is ridiculous."

I rubbed the sleep from my eyes.

"What are you talking about?"

"The Solarium," he spat. "You destroyed the rose garden. It looks like a wild animal tore through there. I just want to know why."

"I have no idea what you're talking about."

"Really?" He reached toward my tussled hair and pulled a green rose leaf from the tangles.

I looked at the leaf for a long moment.

"I don't know how to explain that, but I swear I didn't do anything to your stupid plants."

"At least give me back my clippers so I can take some cuttings and salvage things."

"I don't have them," I threw my hands up, "because I didn't do it."

"I guess you don't mind if I have a look in your quarters, then?"

"Be my guest."

Mac searched my room for several minutes. As I watched, I seethed with indignance. But when he opened my closet door, the pruning shears clattered to the floor and gleamed in the artificial dawn light.

My hand flew to my chest, fingers splayed out like a fan. I looked at Mac and shook my head. *No,* I mouthed.

Mac lifted the shears aloft with a triumphant look and crossed the room toward the door.

I tried to defend myself by suggesting other theories, including the idea that someone else might be roaming about that we don't know about. But Mac just shook his head, told me to get some rest, and left me alone for the rest of the day while he worked on the pod.

I can't tell you how many times I've reread the freezerburn syndrome manual now. And I honestly can't decide which scenario I find more unsettling: The one where there's a third mystery person lurking about on the ship, or the one where there's a madness skittering in the shadows of my own mind.

***

Danica's Log, December 23. Evening.

Mac said the best thing for my recovery from cryo would be to rest in my room, but I have two opposing arguments: A: He's not my mother; and B: I was never the obedient type anyway. While he was busy working on my pod, I slipped out and talked to N.A.N.C.Y. again. There's definitely something going on with my security permissions. I can't even get the most basic information from that blasted machine.

I searched the halls of TALUS-IQ for a third mystery person until I was winded and red in the face. I even took a flashlight with me into air vents and crawled around for as long as my knees could stand it. If there's someone else hiding in here with us, I'm determined to find them.

If there's not another person doing this to me? Well, let's just hope the pieces of my mind aren't too scattered to put back together.

***

Danica's Log, December 24. Evening.

Things became a little stilted between Mac and me since the pruning shears incident, so I decided to treat him to a homecooked meal as an olive branch. He'd mentioned the other day that he hadn't eaten something not straight from a package in years, so I made a simple soup along with my great-great grandmother's pirozhki. I set up a table in the Thornton Lounge and removed the empty extra chairs because it depressed me to be reminded of how many others there should have been walking about when I woke up. My movements echoed in the drafty, open space. The gleaming metal walls should have been reassuring in their strength against the terrors of open space, but instead, they felt severe and unyielding. I wasn't sure what to think of Mac, but even so, I found myself with a growing sense of panic whenever he wasn't around. The loneliness of space is infinite.

So, at first, my relief was palpable when Mac arrived. He'd fetched a deep-red wine and turned music on. As he poured, the steady notes of Beethoven's Sonata Number 8, Pathétique wove a tapestry of greater meaning through the air, and I felt my cheeks flush with a mix of annoyance and embarrassment. He thought it was a date.

What was he thinking? That I'd be interested in a one-night stand right before returning to cryostasis? It was ridiculous.

"So, I happened upon the airlock door the other day and saw a recent record on the screen," I gave him a meaningful look. "What on earth have you been doing over there?"

Mac looked shaken for the first time since I'd met him. His gray eyes wavered.

"I've been throwing out trash."

Hundreds of pounds of trash, I thought.

"What kind of trash?"

"Just trash. You make more of it than you think, just living."

"You know that space littering is becoming a big problem, right? We have an incinerator for that."

He took a savage bite of pirozhki and pinned me with a hard gaze. "Why are you questioning my every move? You're the one sneaking out at night doing who-knows-what. First, it was my garden. And you don't think I hear you crawling through the vents like an animal?"

My spoon froze in midair. Words pooled in my throat but got stuck. I was wound as tight as the wine corkscrew had been.

The polite veneer on Mac's countenance, the flirtatiousness, the playfulness: it all had disappeared.

"Turn the music off." The loud screech of a violin tore through the air as I took my aching head in my hands.

He ignored my comment about the music and took a delicate sip of soup. His impassiveness released my rage.

"I didn't lay a finger on your precious plants. I am *crawling through the vents like an animal* because I am trying to find out who else could be doing these things." I struggled to keep the tremor in my voice under control. "Who knows what else they could be capable of?"

The hard veil over his features fell away and he set his spoon down. His gaze softened.

"Hey, I was just kidding about the vents. I didn't realize my joke would make you so upset. And the garden thing is water under the bridge, okay? Danica, you make a wonderful soup, but this cryostasis has made you a bit paranoid."

My face flushed with embarrassment and I rubbed the back of my neck.

"I know. And I'm sorry. This place is getting to me. It's so quiet—like the whole colony is dead, but I'm stuck here wandering the halls like a little lost ghost. Whenever I'm alone, I almost feel invisible. Does that make any sense?"

He put a light hand on my shoulder. "Danica Burakova, you are many things, but one thing you are certainly not, is *invisible*."

I laughed and released some of the tension building in my shoulders. "Thanks for that."

"So, what's the occasion?" He gestured toward the meal with his spoon.

"Well, I had a little chat with N.A.N.C.Y. yesterday and I noticed it was December 23rd, so I thought we could at least have something special for a Christmas Eve dinner today."

Two little creases of concern appeared between his eyebrows. "Christmas Eve?"

"Yeah," I said, stuffing my mouth full of another bite of Pirozhki. "Didn't your family celebrate it?"

When Mac spoke again his words were slow and measured. "Danica, today is March 3rd, 2301."

I nearly choked on the Pirozhki. "That's impossible. I remember what N.A.N.C.Y. said. Today's Christmas Eve."

"You mean you don't remember the last two months?" He cocked his head to the side with a sad look.

"I..." My heart thundered in my chest. "I don't believe you." I didn't understand my own mind or what I was feeling. Was I afraid? Angry? Embarrassed? My voice became tremulous and tight, and I balled my hands into fists. The tempo of Beethoven's sonata raced out of control in time with my heart. Violins screeched and plucked and picked. "How can anyone remember anything with this damn music wailing in their ears!"

He tapped a paper napkin to his lips. "It's barely on, Danica. But if you insist."

With a soft click, the room went completely still and silent. It was somehow worse without the thin barrier of Beethoven between us.

"Please don't take this the wrong way, but extreme memory loss like this is another sign of serious freezerburn syndrome. Have you been noticing anything else strange lately?"

My lip trembled, but I made myself speak. "I don't have freezerburn syndrome. I don't. You're wrong about the date."

"Danica, calm yourself. I think it's time to go back to your room and rest for a while. You've overexerted yourself."

"No! There's no way I just forgot two months of my life. Let's go to N.A.N.C.Y. right now and ask for the date. I know what I saw."

"Danica, don't do this again. You do this every day." He looked almost embarrassed for me and his eyes were pleading.

I ignored him and stalked to the nearest N.A.N.C.Y. console. I punched my question into the machine.

March 3, 2301, stared right back at me.

I collapsed to my knees. I had lost my mind. Two months of my life were completely wiped from my memory. I wept hot, desperate tears.

Mac approached from behind. He spoke softly next to my ear, like a devil on my shoulder.

"And do you know why N.A.N.C.Y. won't answer your other questions, Danica? The ones you sneak over here to ask when you think I'm not paying attention?"

Curling inward, I hugged my knees and tried to block him out.

He pressed on, his voice resolute. "Before you went into cryosleep, you were on probation from your engineering role. You made one too many mistakes, and you're now on reduced security clearance."

It was all too much. Everything I thought I knew had been turned upside down.

"No. It can't be true," I shrank away from him.

"And yet it is."

I locked my bleary eyes on his, searching for a sign that it was all just another joke.

"I'm sorry." He gray eyes didn't waver.

The truth is that I have no memory of getting disciplinary action. I don't remember having my security clearance revoked. I have memories of pay raises and awards. But something must have happened to revoke my clearance.

You're not supposed to put people back into cryosleep when they have freezerburn syndrome. There's a high likelihood of not waking up the second time. And now I understand why it's been two months and I am still not back in cryosleep: I have freezerburn syndrome, and Mac can't in good conscience put me back under while I'm in this condition.

Two whole months forgotten. It's no longer a question of fixing my pod—it's a question of fixing *me*.

***

Danica's Log. March 4, 2301? Morning, I think.

I can't keep the days straight. I wrote December 25th on this entry at first but had to cross it out. It feels like December 25th, but apparently it isn't. Merry Frickin' Christmas, I guess.

There were eggs in the Pirozhki. I didn't know Mac was allergic. Maybe he told me about the allergy and I forgot. I don't remember. I think I almost killed him. Thankfully, he was aware enough to grab an EpiPen before he succumbed.

Now he's in his room, sick with nausea and diarrhea. Moaning like a wounded animal. I feel a little bad, but also relieved that he's out of my hair for a day.

Since Mac confronted me about my sanity, I've been thinking about my family a lot, since those are some of the only memories I can trust. My papa had this old saying, *In a quiet pond, devils dwell*. I can't stop thinking about that saying and how it conjures the image of Mac's steady gray eyes. My mama had her own saying whenever I broke down in front of her: *Take yourself into your hands*. And I suppose that's all any of us can do, isn't it? Sane or not, we can take ourselves into our own hands and deal with the consequences. I've decided to try that one last time.

I'm sure a prerequisite of losing your mind is not knowing that you've lost it. But still, I want to believe that I'm sane. Now's my chance to swipe Mac's security pass and see if he's hiding something. He's too busy puking his guts out to notice me slip in his room like a little ghost.

***

CHAT LOG SESSION WITH Nonintellectual Answer Network for Crew Year version - 2300 (N.A.N.C.Y)

Soundless, I snuck into Mac's room and got the security pass. Turns out that N.A.N.C.Y.'s a lot friendlier when she thinks she's talking to Mac.

When N.A.N.C.Y scanned the security pass and played the acceptance chime, I sighed with relief.

December 25, 2300.

N.A.N.C.Y: Identity verified. Welcome, Mac Fogarty. Please note that this is not an artificial intelligence. We are an unintelligent chat system, built for query and response.

Danica: Personnel profile for Mac Fogarty.

N.A.N.C.Y: Mac Fogarty, Head of Pod Maintenance for year 2300, Age 25.

An image of Mac appeared before me. Except it wasn't Mac. Not the one I knew, anyway. Walnut-brown eyes and a shaved head. Tan skin and a full, reddish beard. A scowl of concentration where the disarming smile should have been.

Danica: I want to report an error.

N.A.N.C.Y: Thank you for noting an error in our programming. Please complete the attached form.

(With typing sounds): "Error description: Incorrect photo attached to Mac Fogarty's profile. Logs attached."

N.A.N.C.Y.: Thank you for your report. Cross-checking now...

N.A.N.C.Y.: No error detected.

Danica: That picture is not Mac Fogarty, you useless piece of junk.

N.A.N.C.Y.: Thank you so much for using N.A.N.C.Y., an unintelligent chat system. Goodbye.

Danica: Wait.

Danica: Personnel records for Danica Burakova.

N.A.N.C.Y.: Danica Burakova, life systems engineer. In Good Standing.

I nearly shouted with joy. I knew I hadn't been on probation.

Danica: What's the date today?

N.A.N.C.Y.: Today is December 25, 2300. For some, the celebration of Christmas.

The bottom dropped out of my stomach. Had I not lost two months of memory after all?

Danica: System activity for Mac Fogarty during the last week.

N.A.N.C.Y.: Loading historical activity data for Mac Fogarty...

To the average person's eyes, the report would have appeared to be gibberish, but lucky for me, I was an engineer and was used to reading lines of code. A timeline of suspicious activities appeared before my eyes.

On December 20th, 2300, Mac Fogarty's card was used to remove my security clearance. On the very next day, the log showed that Mac's card had been used to set pod 329, my pod, to manual maintenance mode and to initiate the thawing process. Finally, a temporary date override was enacted on December 24th, so that N.A.N.C.Y. would report aloud that the date was March 3, 2301 just once before reverting back to the correct date again.

I stopped breathing. He had been in the system messing around with the manual settings and altering my sense of reality.

I asked N.A.N.C.Y. for the full diagnostic history for pod 329, and all the machine health scans for Pod 329 since the beginning of its recorded existence said the same thing: *system completely functional, energy consumption optimal.*

My god, I whispered. There had never been anything wrong with my pod. He'd planned everything ahead of time and waited for me with a fresh shave. He'd been the shadow darkening my door, weaving rose leaves in my hair at night and questioning my sanity during the day.

I continued to pelt N.A.N.C.Y. with questions. I was sure that I was close to getting to the root of things now.

Danica: How many pods are empty right now?

N.A.N.C.Y.: Currently, there are three empty pods.

I swallowed. There was a hard lump in my throat.

Danica: Who are the empty pods assigned to?

N.A.N.C.Y.: Mac Fogarty, Danica Burakova, and Cyrus Huxley.

Cyrus Huxley. I whispered the name to myself.

Danica: Personnel profile for Cyrus Huxley.

N.A.N.C.Y.: Cyrus Huxley, Head of Pod Maintenance for year 2299, Age 37.

An image appeared, and it was the man I'd spent these last few nightmarish days with: a man with sandy hair, cold gray eyes, and an easy smile.

Danica: Can you show me video surveillance from the last time the airlock was used?

In the recording, Cyrus Huxley, the man who'd called himself Mac Fogarty, struggled with the *real* Mac Fogarty until he subdued him. Cyrus split the man's head open on the floor and then dragged his limp body into the airlock. The body was expelled like trash shortly after.

I knew that the pod maintenance crew had a rolling schedule where they each had a year of our voyage that they were responsible for being awake during. But when his turn in charge was over, it appeared that Cyrus Huxley hadn't been ready to go back to sleep. Despite the horrific situation I found myself in, I felt almost exultant. I was sane, and I had real proof. I felt generous enough to give N.A.N.C.Y. a proper goodbye.

Danica: I'm sorry I called you a bitch, N.A.N.C.Y. You're not a bitch.

N.A.N.C.Y.: There are no female canines currently presiding on TALUS-IQ.

Danica: Aw, N.A.N.C.Y. That's the sweetest thing you've ever said to me.

***

Danica's log, December 25, Evening.

After my chat with N.A.N.C.Y. I rushed to the repository where the multitude of pods waited. I wanted to see Mac and Cyrus' empty pods with my own eyes. I pressed the release button on privacy screen after privacy screen, peering into serene, dreamlike faces through the glass.

But after going through at least a dozen rows of peaceful sleepers, I opened a privacy screen to find the woman inside was not sleeping peacefully. Her face was blue with the pallor of death, and a deep purple bruise crossed her throat. I recoiled, my heart in my throat, not sure if I was more afraid that she was actually dead, or that she would suddenly open her eyes and stare back at me.

She was the first. After her I discovered half a dozen others. Women who all looked to be around my age. All now beyond the reach of sleep and dreams. One's face was so badly beaten that parts of her flesh fluttered up from her cheek in time with the fluid circulation of her pod. Others had long gashes cut into their throats, and the cryogenic solution around them was stained pink. And each with an unmistakable token pinned to her lifeless chest: a rose with a cascade of sun-bright yellow petals swirling down to a necrotic-black frill, speckled as if tossed in a sea of white stardust. *Celestial Dusk* roses. Just like the one slowly unwinding its petals in my room.

Bruises that would never heal. Flesh that would never decay. Women kept in cryostasis as trophies. Cyrus had captured these women, even in death, under cloches of glass. They were like enchanted roses that would never grow into their fullness and be denied even the natural dignity of decay.

I stumbled back to my pod in a dreamlike state, trembling all over and drawn to the red maintenance light. The only one on the entire ship. I reached out and touched it. Still shaking, I then turned in the direction of the nearest N.A.N.C.Y. station, only a few yards away. Using Mac's pass, I asked N.A.N.C.Y. to turn the manual maintenance mode off.

The maintenance light on my pod turned green. As green and vibrant as Russia's steppes in spring. I wept at the sight of it. That's how close I had been the entire time. All the time when Cyrus had been in here cursing and bellowing at the machine, it had been an act to convince me he was doing something. I knew I wouldn't be going back to cryosleep but seeing that gorgeous green light filled me with a sense of accomplishment all the same.

I knew at that moment that there was no way around it: I wasn't the first to be murdered, and I was next in line. Even if I don't make it, I'm going to do all I can to save *you*.

This is the most important part, so pay attention. I contaminated the coffee maker he uses, the one with the yellow sticker, with raw egg whites. I did this for you, to give you time and a fighting chance. With any luck, he'll use it.

I also hid the EpiPens in the air vent in Vestibule A. I'm sure people will need them eventually when you all wake up.

I hear distant footsteps. He must be feeling better. I don't have much time before he comes for me. I'll try my best to get the bastard, but he outsizes me, and my muscles are still weakened from being in cryo.

I just remembered the bird I saw with the cold, persistent eyes like his. It was an eagle. Have you ever seen how an eagle hunts for fish? It swoops down from the air and scoops one right out of the water with its talons. It's not a fair kind of fight, as I'm sure the fish never even saw it coming.

Don't be the fish.

P.S. - If you manage to make it back to your pod, can you tell my family I love them when you all wake up together?

***

After reading the letter, the pages drop from your hands. There are goosebumps on your skin even though you've long since warmed up from cryostasis.

As you stare at the ceiling, memories of your awakening flood your mind with diamond-bright clarity: The man who had been waiting for you with his disheveled shirt and crimson face. Juniper mingled with the sour smell of sweat filling your nostrils. His swollen lips. Hives on his skin under his sandy hair. Despite feeling your own disorientation, you'd had a near-immediate desire to help and began running through diagnostic criteria in your mind. After all, as a medic for the TALUS-IQ, it was your job to help in any medical emergency.

As you had looked into his gray eyes, his swollen lips parted and a pink-tinged strand of spittle spilled down from a gap where he was missing a tooth. His hands were clasped and his forearms were covered in bright red scratches. The man took each breath with monumental effort, but still, he had spoken to you.

Grotesque and lopsided though it had been, he had also grinned at you. It had been hard to understand his words because of the thinness of his voice and the way his swollen tongue had tripped over the words. Still, you had been able to make out at least one sentence:

"Hey there, Sleeping Beauty. You're finally awake."

***

Note: An altered version of this story was originally produced on the Nighty Night with Rabia Chaudry podcast.

2

Wavetouched

Summer, and the coral bands were wrong. Well, not *wrong* exactly, because they couldn't be anything other than what they were—bands of growth showing the swell and abatements of the years. Still, the patterns, which for the merpeople had always been a source of divination, were not as expected. Calamity, the prophet of the wave, locked the brittle specimen in a labeled compartment. She swam back and eyed the last ten years through boxes of coral. Change was happening, but whatever had caused it, Calamity hadn't predicted it in time. The plague was already here.

Her mind's eye still fixed upon the image of brittle, faded coral, Calamity continued to her next and final responsibility of the day—ministering to the imprisoned. There was just one prisoner at the moment, and the teenage mer in the underwater jail cell was the only thing stopping Calamity from continuing her vigil at her dying niece's bedside. Eager to get it over with, she swam straight toward the jail. Once she arrived, she entered with only a perfunctory nod in the guard's direction.

The prisoner wasn't from her territory. You could tell by the loose brown hair floating and twisting around his face, obscuring him like a patch of thick seaweed. The rest of him, including a shining silver tail, rested belly-down on a small recessed slab of gray stone. The longhair people had always seemed as wild as their untamed hair, but usually the boundaries of territory made it rare to encounter one.

A long, red gash bisected the youth's silver tailfin, right below his green torso. Calamity frowned, wondering if someone had been too rough with him during the arrest. He was still just a boy, especially to someone in their middle years like her. His chin, what she could see of it at least, rested in his hands in a childlike fashion. He sat up when he saw her, and she sighed without meaning to. She was tired.

The boy's eyes went wide as he approached the bars. "Your eyes are white as sand dollars." He took in her admittedly daunting appearance, his eyes lingering with curiosity on the silver sigils tattooed on her bare scalp.

Calamity looked back and glimpsed sharp, intelligent amber eyes between strands of sandy brown hair. He opened his mouth as if to speak again, but before he could say anything, Calamity made the motions of the Wave with her long gray fingers.

Her eyes had always been unique, even among her own people. But long ago she had tired of being marveled at. Some mer seemed to make the mistake of thinking that looking special indicated depth of character. In truth, aside from contrasting nicely with the black shell garlands wrapped around her waist, the color of her eyes meant nothing. More often, it was an unwelcome distraction in her line of work. The rest of her body, tailfin and all, was slate gray. Only her eyes broke the hegemony of plainness.

"May the Wave cleanse you and make you whole," she finished, scooping a fold of water with her tail fin and throwing it in the young man's direction. She turned and swam toward the exit.

"Wait!" The teenager exclaimed.

Calamity gritted her teeth. "You've been blessed. Good night, son of the Wave."

"You're a holy merwoman, right?"

Calamity scowled. Her greatest dream had been to hear the voice of the Wave itself whispering in her ears. Years of incessant prayer had failed to reveal the secret to her. Worse still, the plague arrived last year, ravaging the lives of innocents and evildoers alike, shaking what little faith she'd held on to. Seeing her niece fall to it despite the rituals and prayers of protection had been the deepest cut of all. Calamity had resigned herself to the life of a false prophet, keeping her doubts concealed.

She shrugged. "I am Lady Calamity, the prophet of The Wave."

"That sounds important. Maybe you'll be smart enough to listen."

"You are brazen, even for a longhair."

"All I want is for someone to listen."

As soon as the word *listen* left the boy's lips, the base of Calamity's skull tingled. She whirled around, but there was nothing behind her but her own gray tailfin. As much as she wanted to rush back to her niece's bedside, there was something in this teenager's voice that stopped her cold. Her intuition became as loud as seagull screams.

"I'm listening," she said.

"Our people are dying. The waters have warmed. The coral fades, shrivels, and dies. We have no fish and we have no food."

Calamity crossed her arms and flared her gills. "You told us all this during your ravings when you assaulted the king."

"I only tugged his sleeve! And I never got to the important part."

Calamity looked at the boy, probably no more than sixteen, and felt pity. "If you show remorse, I can speak to the king about your release."

"You are the ones who should show remorse," he growled. There was a roaring fire in his brown eyes.

She shrank back despite the bars between them.

"I keep trying to tell you people. There's nothing left for me back home. It's too late for all of us unless we can find refuge. We cannot traverse farther than your hunting territory without dying of hunger."

"And if we take you in, you'll all die of the plague. Is that what you want?"

His face darkened. "The world is changing. Don't you feel it? How do you know that the very same warming that killed our coral isn't the reason why your people are overwhelmed by the plague? It could be all the waters of the whole world."

"This is outrageous," Calamity said, hiding her growing fear behind a front of anger. "Why send a child diplomat, if the situation is so dire?"

"My people didn't send me," he said. "They said it would be hopeless to deal with you. But I had to do something. Don't you see that you'll be next? The only way to survive the future is by banding together."

"What you say holds some truth," Calamity conceded in a soft voice. "But you young merpeople love to speak of utopias and ideals, while the experienced among us have lived long enough to know how such attempts end. We have our own tragedy to look after." She swallowed hard. "My niece is dying of plague."

"I'm sorry. What's your niece's name?"

"Iyana." She found herself saying the name with a wincing expression as if already grieving the girl's death before it even happened.

"What if I could cure Iyana and all those like her?" he said fervently.

"I'd crown you king myself," she scoffed. "Because it would be a miracle."

"We have a cure for the plague. We'll exchange it for refuge and shelter."

Calamity felt her gills flare. "Don't lie to me."

"I can prove it," he pleaded.

Calamity was about to say no, but a vivid picture of her four-year-old niece came to her. The girls' sweet, rounded cheeks had shriveled to sharp planes over the last months, and the girl's pain had become excruciating and relentless. This week, blood had started to seep from her gills, and Calamity's hope was emptying in a similar fashion.

"How?" she heard herself ask.

"Set me free, and I'll return with the cure."

Calamity laughed bitterly. "If only I were so naïve. If it's all dying out, why would you give away something so precious?"

"It's as good as gone already. Someone might as well use it before it's gone. If I don't come back in the morning, what will you lose?"

"My niece, possibly," she said in a whisper. "She's dying. Can this coral cure her?"

"Yes. Why do you think the plague never took hold in our territory?"

"I will personally hunt you down and drag you back if you do not return," she said in a hoarse whisper. "And if your coral doesn't cure her, you'll rot in prison."

"It'll work," the boy said. "No need for threats. And when it works, you'll give my people a home."

It was still hard to see his face through the cloud of hair, but she caught a glimpse of his eyes under bushy brown eyebrows. An earnest gleam spoke of deep purpose.

"Or that make-me-king thing also sounded pretty good."

The corners of her lips curled up. "If your cure works, I'll invite your people in with open arms," she replied. "What is your name, you foolish thing?"

"Titan," he said, grinning.

Calamity went to the guard and informed him that she would be keeping vigil with the youth that night, ministering to the misguided soul. The guard practically skipped away, glad to be given the night off.

Her hands shook as she opened the door to the boy's jail cell. "You'd better come back. Our futures rest on you."

"Everyone told me it was hopeless, but maybe your Wave thing is real. You're different." He shot out with a few flicks of his tail and was gone with the enviable swimming speed that only the young possess.

Calamity stood in the empty stone room for a long time after, hugging herself. She couldn't stop thinking about what the teenager had said about the Wave. Even if it was real, which she didn't believe anymore, she no longer felt worthy of its favor. It was Calamity who'd selfishly convinced her sister to take little Iyana out to Calamity's worship services even with the plague creeping across their community.

"You can't live in fear. The Wave will protect the faithful," Calamity had said to her sister. Now, with Iyana swimming steadily toward the gates of death, Calamity felt daily the weight of guilt. Not only for Iyana's fate, but for Calamity's sin against all those faithful who had trusted in the Wave's protection and still had fallen sick.

***

There was another floater in the sickbay. The dead merman's body pressed against the ceiling of the cave like a lost balloon. Calamity found herself drawn into his blank gray eyes and felt her stomach turn as she watched a string of old mucous and blood stretch away from his mouth like a river frozen in time. A nurse approached and yanked on the dead mer's tail. She slung a weighted sheet over his corpse and shoved the bundle out of the way. His body pressed up against its covering, the fabric swelling up like a boil as he rose.

"Here to see Iyana?" The nurse said. "She's sleeping for once, poor dear. Try not to wake her when you go in. She should dream the day away instead of suffering."

Calamity nodded, afraid she would gag if she opened her mouth. Even though she visited daily, the pungent odor of blood, vomit, and shit still rankled as if it was the first time. She pulled one of the wide ribbons of her garment loose and held it over her nose as they swam through the gauntlet of groans, moans, and screams from multitudes of bedridden sick.

The nurse departed as soon as they were at Iyana's bed. The plague doctor was there, and turned his head, seeming to watch Calamity through his pointed mask. His barbed tail curved behind him as she approached.

His mask reminded her of a carrion bird she once saw picking at a beached whale. She felt the instinct to shoo him away lest he devour the girl. And he would undoubtedly challenge Calamity if he witnessed her administer some kind of mystery treatment.

She aimed a level gaze at the bird-like mask. "I need to be alone with Iyana to perform my rites. They are not for your eyes."

The doctor turned and made for the next patient, not even uttering a word. As soon as he turned his back, she pulled the heavy curtain around to conceal the bed from view, arranging the large stone weights with care. When she was satisfied with the level of privacy, she turned to her dying niece.

The nurse had been right. Calamity had come during one of Iyana's better times. Normally, Iyana rolled from side to side in pain as she thrashed and coughed and grabbed at whoever stood next to the bed, begging for the pain to end.

Instead of the usual horror, Iyana slept. Her brow looked pale but she was quite flushed in her cheeks. The blood in her neck bloomed near the surface in uneven splotches. Calamity felt tears burn in her eyes as she saw how bony and frail her little gray wrist was, nothing like the plump little thing she'd been before the plague. Iyana's short and labored breaths had long pauses between them, her gills sluggish, as if they were sucking in thick mud rather than water. In the water, a cloud of pink mucous floated above the girl's head like a halo, and Calamity swiped it away.

"Iyana," she whispered, rousing the girl. "You need to take some medicine."

The girl's eyes fluttered open and her bleary gaze landed on her aunt. The blood vessels in her eyes had burst from coughing and vomiting.

"What medicine?" she rasped.

"With any luck," Calamity said as she held the brain coral aloft, "a cure. But this has to be a secret for now. Don't tell anyone."

The little girl nodded and opened her bluish, cracked lips.

The coral before her seemed to have so many paths cut into its skin, all winding and curving, some converging. There was no one true path—only endless meandering.

***

"You will tell no mer of this cure," the king said, his face dark with anger. "There will be no deal with the longhair." His heavy metal circlet glinted from the top of his bald head. "Perhaps it's the Wave's way of testing and fishing out the weak."

Calamity balled her hands into tight fights. She could not speak.

"You may go," the king said, waving her away.

Calamity lowered herself to the floor, pleading with him. "The death groans of children cannot be that which the Wave wills. The weak are not expendable. They're ours to protect."

"I'm sure you agree, Lady Calamity, that the Wave has a will of its own. In this case, we should not meddle in it." He rubbed his forehead as if she'd annoyed him greatly. "If anyone finds out there's a cure, you'll just add unrest to our many problems. We must keep a united front. We will arise from the ocean floor with only those who were strong enough to withstand the disease. Perhaps the next generation will be immune."

Calamity clasped her hands together so hard the knuckles went white. This was not what she had expected. Perhaps, in her wildest fantasies, she thought that after telling the king about her niece's miraculous recovery, she'd be crowned a hero. *Lady Calamity: Banisher of Plague*, would be her legacy. But this? She'd never dreamed of the king outlawing a cure.

"Just so I understand correctly: the command of my king is to let everyone die," she said, her voice shaking, "because the cost of salvation is too great."

"No," the king said, banging his trident on the stone floor, "the command of the king is to protect the future for the survivors."

She felt the warm trickle of her tears join the surrounding waters. "I cannot keep such a secret. My niece was dying and now she's cured!"

The king's voice bellowed. "Say it is a miracle! Say she was Wave-touched. Say she never had the plague and it was something else entirely. I don't care what you say as long as you do not speak of a cure."

Calamity's hands trembled. Despite her doubts, she now felt a fierce protectiveness over the faith that held many of her people in its embrace. To imply that she should lie about such a thing as being Wavetouched was tantamount to making a mockery of their culture. She understood now that the king cared nothing about whether his people lived or died, as long as comfort, the status quo, and, most importantly, *he* remained unchallenged.

She swallowed and bowed her head. "If that is all, your highness." As she swam out of the throne room, she heard the king's still-enraged voice at her back.

"Do not mistake the peoples' reverence for power, Lady Calamity. Your head is severed from its body just as easily as anyone else's." At this, there was a small motion of the last three of the king's fingers as he flicked his eyes at his right-hand guard.

Before Calamity understood what was happening, the king's attendant, a young man of just eighteen, was seized by the guard as another swept out his great axe. The axe made a wide arc and severed the man's head from his shoulders. The head floated up quickly to the ceiling, making bobbing circles of blood as it went. The body was more reluctant, following more slowly. The body's tailfin continued to twitch and jerk for a few torturous seconds after it had been separated. Calamity had the absurd thought, no doubt born of shock, that the young man had the most beautiful scales she'd ever seen. A death dance of light glinted from the ornate royal lamps, illuminating the fuscia hues of dead mer's scales.

The king sought out her eyes, banging his jeweled scepter on the floor. The sound pierced through Calamity's trance as it echoed in the cavernous space.

"I am loathe to kill a prophet of a wave," The king said, still pinning her with his gray eyes. "I allow you to stand, only because I trust you can keep a secret. And the people would not take kindly to losing you. Consider this a confessional room. And the coral is my confession."

Calamity realized she'd been holding the base of her neck and moved her hands down. She shook so much that it was difficult for one hand to find the other as she clasped them at her belly. She performed a gesture that she hoped looked like a nod, but as she felt the swell of nausea in her stomach, the movement became more like a curling of her whole body.

"And if you cannot my confession keep..." He trailed off.

Calamity raised her gaze to the ceiling, where at least a dozen heads collected in the apex of the dome-shaped ceiling, all in varying states of decay. In addition to the decapitated heads, bones and lumps of swollen flesh were nibbled upon by schools of small fish that darted back and forth in silver flashes.

She jetted out of the room, and only in the cave-like foyer of stone, in a lonely dark corner, did she dare stop to catch her breath, rub her prayer beads, and release the contents of her stomach.

The plague had changed everything, and this had been the worst change of all.

The King is mad. We've lost the king.

***

The boy's eyes were bright when Calamity returned to his cell. "It worked, didn't it!" he shouted.

"Yes."

"Then what's wrong?" he asked, his eyes narrowing in confusion as Calamity leaned her head against the bars with a pained expression. She said nothing for a long time.

"The king doesn't want a cure. He would rather sentence us to death instead of take in your people. He forbade me from telling anyone about the cure." She decided to leave out the part about the beheading.

The boy said grabbed the bars, thrusting his head through. "You can't just quit! Think of all the people who will die."

"And what shall I do? Be killed?" she replied.

"Who's to say the plague won't kill you anyway?" The boy reared back and threw his hands up in the water.

"It probably will," she replied, shaking her head. "There is too much animosity between our tribes. The king will never listen."

"But what if the king *has* to listen?" he said, his eyes ablaze with purpose again. "If you told the people that there was a cure, they would never let him withhold it. They trust you, don't they? I can tell. It's the same reason I trusted you. Lady Calamity, forgive me, but I think if there is a Wave, it put you here for this."

It was true that the people trusted her. Never once had she spoken out against the king. Never once had she even given a hint about her wavering faith in the Wave. She had stored up enough quiet power for one explosive act.

Before she could lose courage, she flung open his cell door. "Go home, you foolish boy!" she commanded.

"Why?" he said, unmoving. "I'll die of hunger there anyway."

"Because I'm about to make the worst mistake of my life, but perhaps it can fix some of the other messes I've made." She made the sacred sign of the Wave and began a blessing in his direction. A parting gesture. Her motions were stopped by the boy's sudden hug. She patted him on the head. In another life, she imagined they could have been friends. Perhaps she would have mentored him. But Calamity would never mentor anyone now.

"But the Wave *will* like what you do, won't it?" he said with a small grin as he made for the exit.

"I hope so," she whispered. "I don't know what the Wave wants anymore. I think..." She was surprised by a sudden choking feeling in her throat that stopped her from speaking.

"That we have to trust our own hearts?" the boy finished.

Calamity nodded and turned the boy's shoulders so that he was facing the exit and gave him a rough push out.

***

Calamity waited to be taken away. Curiously, it was taking longer than expected. She'd charged her sister with spreading the word about the coral. She wondered how many knew by now. Hopefully enough to spread to everyone. Otherwise, this might all be for nothing.

Silence and calm reigned in the pitch black of the castle grounds. Waiting in a thick clump of seagrass, Calamity feared that her plan hadn't worked. Perhaps her hires had been captured already, their heads the latest leaking bobbles on the king's ceiling. She rubbed her prayer beads so hard that the string broke, sending white beads and shells floating around her body. Carefully, she swiped each one out of the water and clutched them tight in her hands. Only one had escaped her reach, and it floated high above her. In an illusion of space and distance, it looked like a little white moon above the dark stone castle.

Finally, she could breathe again when she saw the pale streamers of red water she'd been waiting for. The castle had four imposing towers and at least a dozen windows were facing the front grounds where she skulked. It didn't happen all at once, but window by window, the castle began to bleed. Each time, the blood was predicated by the snuffing out of the warm yellow light. There was no sound to it.

Calamity regarded this gruesome work of her own doing in awe. As the blood curled out from the king's royal balcony, the red royal banner draped over the side became lost in the dark pigments. Perhaps it was mere horror and shock at having paid for the assassins with offerings from the penitent, but another absurd thought came to her as she watched the last light in the castle wink out.

Kingdoms don't scream when they die—they just blink and bleed.

But that wasn't true, was it? There were enough screams in the sick bay for an entire generation. When still nobody came to get her, Calamity decided to surface then and feel the crisp night air on her skin. The waves rolled over her numb body as she used her fin to hover at the surface, watching the bloodied foam amass. It was pink. Pink as the mouth on Ayana's favorite doll.

3

Snowdrifter

Gregory was convinced that some *lowlife drifter*, as he put it, was roaming our remote property in northern Michigan. The evidence? A set of medium-sized human footprints that appeared nightly on the snowbanks leading to our cabin. The steps went up to the window, then back out toward the pines. But Gregory and I disagreed on the intentions of our visitor. I didn't think they were some *lowlife*. Whoever traversed the forest at night had to have been freezing to death. Maybe, I thought, they just lacked the nerve to ask to come inside. Perhaps this person needed our help.

While Gregory stalked the hills during the day under the excuse of hunting, I knew that he was actually looking for the owner of the footsteps. What he planned to do with the person when he caught them, I didn't know. But it was the first time in our month-long marriage that I had seen this side of Gregory. He was obsessed, snarling, and distant whenever the topic of our visitor came up.

Tonight, I decided to do a little of my own hunting. When I heard Gregory's breathing broken by a rhythm of snores, I slipped out from the heavy plaid coverlet. There had never been a time in our relationship before that I'd hid anything from him. But my instincts told me that if he knew what I was doing, he'd try to stop me. And I couldn't let him stop me. Somebody needed my help.

Slogging through the glistening snow, I waited in a spot by the cabin that gave shelter from the wind. Right when I began to despair that my presence had scared off the visitor for good, I saw a disturbance in the snow. Before my widened eyes, the snow crunched down on itself as if molding around the shape of a human foot. Alone, that was unremarkable. But there were no feet to be seen. No human visitor to observe. The footsteps continued to appear in the wake of some invisible being, leading into the desolate pine forest. Drops of red punctuated the bottom of the footsteps, hissing with heat as the blood struck snow.

I raced after the prints until they stopped in the middle of a clearing. Snow flew as I dug my gloved hands through the white ground, suspecting but not sure of what I'd find. Under the snow was a small, flat tombstone, belonging to an *Avelina* who shared my new husband's last name. The date of her death was listed as the day before my own marriage to Gregory.

I tumbled back into the snowdrift I'd made. Gregory's angry calls rang out into the night, sending a horned owl into the star-strewn sky. Insight dawned on me as I sprinted through ice and snow. Every step left a trail of prints to follow, making a contest of whether I could reach the safety of town before Gregory caught me. The visitor hadn't needed saving—she'd been trying to save *me*.

4

The Popcorn Ceiling

I was twelve when we pulled up to the driveway of a 1970's ranch-style home—one with the kind of brick that had such a pale-yellow cast that it made it seem like something had scared the color right out of them.

"Lovely house," Mom said, putting the car into park. "Things are going to be different here." As she smiled, I imagined that she was really believing it, but I knew better. She'd be hitting the bottle before the week's end.

She sighed, low and loud, and waited quietly for my response.

I narrowed my eyes at the house. Mom hadn't bothered to include me on any of the house-hunting or purchasing activities. It was the first time I'd seen it. For that reason alone, I was determined not to like it.

I licked my dry lips. "There's a gravel drive. Can't play basketball here."

The key ground harshly against the ignition as she yanked it out. "You don't even play basketball."

"Because we never had anywhere to put a hoop."

She rolled her eyes. When her gaze slid back over my face, it was with a flat, empty expression that made me shiver.

"You're a lucky boy to have such a nice house."

You're a lucky woman to get a new job.

I wondered what she'd been fired for this time and how she'd managed to con the new lab into hiring her. The dismissal must have had something to do with alcohol, but I couldn't know exactly how they'd found out about her problem.

We walked through the house with only the busy hum of the central air conditioning breaking the silence between us. Down the main hallway, a guest bathroom and two bedrooms waited like open mouths. The biggest bedroom had dark blue carpet and nothing much to speak of in terms of style. But the guest bedroom was a crime against good taste. There was a lime-green shag rug in a shocking electric hue, and the ceiling was completely plastered in a thick, goopy-looking mess of textured white lumps and bumps.

I wondered what the room had looked like before, when the previous occupant had no doubt had it decked out in their own very groovy style. Beads on the door frame. Peace signs everywhere. Smoke tendrils curling up to the lumpy ceiling.

I looked down the hallway, desperate to find another room that didn't exist.

"I don't want the room with the green carpet and the gross ceiling!" I shouted into the doorway of the biggest bedroom. "Is there anything else?"

My mom silently padded in, standing next to me. I took a reflexive step away from her.

"It's called a popcorn ceiling, and it's very stylish. And the green carpet is very fun!"

"But—"

"Stop whining."

The next few days were a blur of the regular routine that always took hold after moving to a new place: Go to school, get picked on, come home, and fight with mom. For this first week, though, she was sober, so she cooked for us at least. But like the other parts of our new-home routine, I knew that this was just temporary, and it would soon end.

"Apparently, kids bring cupcakes on their birthday at this school too. Like all the others I've been to." I said to her one night when I was feeling brave and crusty. I was fresh from the sting of rejection, my lack of know-how to bring sugared treats had no doubt sealed my fate as the outsider for the year at this school, just like the other schools. I had begged her to let me bring something this time, even if it was just bought from the store.

She forgot.

Mom rolled her eyes. "I'm a researcher. Those other moms probably don't even work. They have time to bake cupcakes all day. You should be proud to have a mother like me doing important things."

"What about me? Am I important?" I asked her. My tone was light and teasing, with a hint of a whine, as if I were like those other kids who complained about things like not getting the latest and greatest video game on release day. Inside, I was cracked and parched, like I was stranded in the desert and waiting for rain.

She sighed. "How can you ask me that? Haven't I already given up everything for you?"

I swallowed hard and watched her silhouette retreat to the main bedroom.

***

Mom was using the I'm-a-very-important-scientist tone with the lab intern she wanted to impress.

She thought that I didn't hear her say "her little life-ruiner" was sick and couldn't go to school today, so please excuse the "distraction." People usually laughed at that because they thought it was a joke.

The white door was propped open, giving me an obvious way to hear the conversation, but mom only remembered me so long as her eyes were directly on me, and once those brown orbs no longer graced me with their attention, I returned to the box of relative obscurity, like a good little boy.

Despite all the pain she'd caused me, I always longed for the attention of mom's cold brown eyes, as if she'd thaw one day and start to function like a normal mom who remembered things like to bring cupcakes to school on your birthday. As if she could warm up over time like an old car in winter.

"Aw, your son looks just like you," cooed the intern. Her name was Sadie. "I wish I had a little carbon-copy like that." Her reddish hair was lit up like a jack-o-lantern with the fluorescent bulbs behind her. She had these beautiful apple-round cheeks with orange-brown freckles rising up like a speckled sunset over her wide smile. I watched but wouldn't speak to her with mom around, because mom was sure to humiliate me somehow.

"You should freeze your eggs," my mom advised the young woman. "I had Alfred much too young. Ruined my career."

Whenever mom spoke about me, like now, I felt her resentment covering me, shrink-wrapping me.

"Spitting image of you though," Sadie said, looking at me.

"Not really," My mom said, her mouth a flat line. "The lighting's dim in here." If the one-directional lighting somehow made Sadie even more beautiful, it made my mother look more skeletal. My mom's eyes were deep, dark voids, her face gaunt and hard. She leaned down to finish the calculation she'd been working on with not even a glance in my direction.

"Don't get any ideas, Sadie," my mom said. "You need to get an IUD and wait until you're in your forties if you want to make it in this career. My career completely stalled when I had a baby."

I looked over to see Sadie's reaction. She was frowning and biting a nail as she studied my face with her large brown eyes. I turned around so she wouldn't see how red I was.

My mother continued speaking as she rifled through a container of pipettes. "This needs your full attention. I don't need to remind you that we need one of these spiders to reproduce to get our funding for another year. I've tried to get the director to extend it, but my petition was denied. We have to figure out how it's done."

Sadie groaned. "How are they supposed to have babies when they keep eating the males?"

"We just have to hope that one of the males got lucky before his luck ran out."

Their voices trailed off as I walked past the red bio-hazard poster and gave it a little punch in the middle, right at the center where there's a target-like circle. A familiar smell, a bit like mom's nail polish remover, wafted into my nose. I tapped the eye-rinse station: front, middle, end.

Then I approached four small terrariums with heat lamps blazing. I went to the first one and peered into the tiny arrangement of leaves and dried grasses. There was a spider somewhere in there, but there was no web. The hand-written label below the terrarium just said female.

I found her on the end of a branch and jumped back on my heels because she blended in perfectly with the brown twigs of her habitat. As I recognized the spider for what it was, her features began to emerge with study: Eight iridescent eyes, eight furry legs, and two obscenely large mandibles.

I knew that my mom had nicknamed this new species the "carpenter spider" because of its sharp jaws that it used for gouging its prey while also injecting it with poison.

I picked up the clear box and felt revulsion and excitement flood me simultaneously. It could have been the most poisonous spider in the world. Nobody knew because it was a newly discovered species. It skittered angrily in the box and my hands trembled at the thought of this small creature's dangerous power.

"Aw," I said. "You've been locked up with nobody but my mom as company."

I looked at the creature as it trembled with a microcosm of rage. It rammed up against the front of the terrarium. I chuckled and stroked the glass as it reared back on its hind legs, mandibles clicking. I tilted my head and considered my options. The case was locked, of course, but the lock was just magnetic and I knew where mom kept the release keys.

When I try to think now of why I was attracted to that spider, it's hard to explain. It was a repulsive creature. Fat, hairy body with long white stripes. A scoop-shaped proboscis that scissored and snapped as it studied me.

The best way I can describe the attraction to that spider was the feeling you get when you press two opposing magnets against each other for the first time. It's thrilling to feel the resistance between the two, and to push them together, feeling the firm push of something invisible pressing out against your actions. It's the closest thing you've ever felt to magic. You know there's science behind it, but that's not what you think about. All you feel is the invisible force, the power.

I wanted that spider like I wanted to press two opposing magnets together, just to feel the raw tension surging and humming between my fingers.

I tapped at the glass and the spider reared back again, snapping its expansive jaws. "Don't worry...You're coming home with me."

Into my backpack she went.

By the time I got to the privacy of my own room and unzipped my backpack, the case was still where I'd stashed it, but the spider was gone. As I turned the clear box over in my hands, I saw a small crack that seemed just barely large enough for it to have escaped. After checking the backpack and the car in a panic, I tore my room apart looking for it. After hours of searching, I slept. I felt the phantom touch of fuzzy legs all night. But when a week had passed and I still hadn't seen it, I assumed it was gone for good. Still, that's when I started the habit of shaking out my shoes and clothes.

***

By the end of that first week, mom was in the bathtub.

It was the worst drinking she did because she almost drowned every time she did it. A particularly bad week would strike her at work. I never understood what problems drove her to do it, but I could feel their weight. She filled the garden tub in the master bathroom, and I covered my eyes as I heard the pipes rattle and groan.

I organized my baseball cards. Tore all the binders apart and flung everything into chaos. Then I smoothed the creases and reorganized them again. After two hours, I went to check on her.

She was slumped in the tub of now-cold water, her nose just barely sticking out for breathing. Two empty bottles of wine flanked the base of the tub like sentries. While averting my eyes, I reached under her back to pull the plug. I grabbed the old ratty towel from the rack and threw it over her as the water drained out.

I went to bed and left my lamp on. I wanted to sleep, but I began to see shapes in the popcorn ceiling as I stared blankly up. There were gelatinous globs that resembled frogs and smaller ones that swam in my peripheral vision like flies. I could have sworn I saw a dark shadow appear in the far corner and then disappear into the white. The faces were the worst. The longer I stared, the more the popcorn ceiling began to spawn personalities. Bulbous eyes that taunted me and fat tongues that lolled out of huge pockmarked mouths. In English class once, we looked at some photos that went with Dante's inferno. I thought that the faces in my ceiling looked a lot like the suffering grimaces in those pictures.

As time passed, I began to feel an impression of hunger emanating from the ceiling. It was like something was lurking in that white roiling sea, waiting to emerge and pull me in. The longer I stared, the more it moved and undulated beneath my gaze. Another lesson came to mind: a mythology lesson on the River Styx. All the illustrations had shown dark, deep waters, but I was sure that it looked more like my ceiling: A white, chalky thing. Viscous and full of horrors.

With great effort, I ripped my eyes away, which helped the nausea that had been building. But what else was there to look at in my room? The lime-green shag carpet? That was almost just as bad as the ceiling.

I closed my eyes tightly and turned the lamp off, closing it all off from view. I decided that I would pretend to be somewhere else. In my pretend world I was actually in a fancy hotel waiting to go to the Yankee Stadium the next day for a baseball game. In my imagination, the sheets were clean and crisp, and there were free snacks and sodas in the mini fridge. My mom wasn't there. It was just me, and it was glorious.

But even with that beautiful scene playing in my mind, I tossed and turned all night, waking up and sweating every hour. I felt tickles on my feet and hands, and more than once had flung the bed covers aside in a panic, only to find nothing at all. The only way I was able to sleep was by throwing the sheets off entirely so that I would know for sure if I felt something.

And it happened just like that every week after that, with my mom and the bathtub and with me and the ceiling.

***

If I thought my mother had been angry about the first sick day when she'd had to bring me into the office, her mood had been angelic compared to the second time I got sick. A week before I got sick, she'd found a single cigarette in my backpack. I'd taken it from another boy who I hoped would befriend me. When he'd offered me a smoke, I was too terrified to lose my only chance at a friend to refuse. I never really intended to use it.

But ever since my mother had found it, it seemed she had something to blame for my inadequate parts, and she made sure to remind me of it every chance she got. My sick day was no exception.

"The smoking has already affected your immune system," she raged on the ride to the lab. "It's probably done permanent damage. Did you know that? Probably not. You didn't have much brains to begin with, and now you've probably got even less. Your body won't ever be the same again. I might as well have kicked back an extra glass of wine or two while I was pregnant with you if I'd known you'd disrespect your body like this. Why did I bother being careful?"

She swung her face toward me briefly, away from the road, her dark eyes pinning me down in my seat like a shadowbox butterfly. I wanted to stand up for myself, but then I smelled the sharp bitterness of alcohol on her rank breath and noted the wild rat's nest of her hair, which she hadn't bothered to brush for work. It was then that I noticed we were weaving slightly toward wherever she directed her attention to.

I clenched my teeth and clutched the seat belt strap.

"I'm sorry, mom," I said, hoping to placate her and get her eyes back on the road.

"Hm," she replied, continuing to weave down the road. But at least her eyes were back on the asphalt now.

After we got to the lab, I did my best to disappear into the background, shuffling my baseball cards and making piles of things I wanted to trade at a school, even though I knew nobody would want to trade with someone like me. I sat on the floor, surrounded by my cards the entire morning. Everything was pretty boring until my mom took her first bathroom break, stumbling out the doors and going toward the bathrooms down the hall.

As soon as the lab doors swung shut, I heard tight little footsteps rushing toward me on the tile. I looked up in alarm and saw Sadie's rosy, freckled face looking down at me with a concentrated little frown.

"Alfred," she whispered in a hoarse voice, casting a furtive glance at the double doors as if she feared my mother's return. "I'm sorry if this is...uncomfortable, but I could never forgive myself if I didn't ask. Is everything okay at home?"

"Uh..." I replied, both dumbstruck by the personal nature of her question and awestruck by seeing her beautiful face up close.

She crossed her arms and looked back at the doors again. "I just can't help but notice that your mother is having...issues."

I swallowed. This time I looked at the doors too. This was my chance. My real chance to get back at my mom that was way better than a snide comment. This could have an actual effect.

My mouth went dry. I felt tears sting the back of my eyes, and I knew I'd cry if I opened my mouth again. I hated myself for it. I knew she was a woman and I was only twelve, but I still wanted to impress her. I couldn't cry in front of her at least.

She bounced on her toes for a moment, then sighed. "I'm sorry. I know it's none of my business. Just...if you need anything, call me, okay? If you get in some kind of trouble at home, or if things get too bad, just call. If you need a safe place to stay during a binge. Help with homework. Anything at all. My dad had the same problem and I can see the signs. It messed me up big time and I—gotta' go. She's coming back."

She slipped a little piece of paper into my palm. Her fingertips were cold. It was a phone number.

My face turned crimson, and I pocketed the note, pretending to study the back of a baseball card again as my mother reappeared.

Sadie washed her hands in the sink next to me for no reason, then returned to the stool where she'd been working on a problem.

That night I couldn't stop thinking about Sadie and her offer. Suddenly, everything in my life that I'd adapted to over my twelve years seemed newly unbearable. I thought of Sadie's words when my mother refused to help me with my make-up homework. I thought of Sadie when my stomach grumbled and I looked at the empty pantry and fridge after my mother became too drunk to cook dinner or drive to the store.

I thought of Sadie's offer when my mother called in sick to work the next day because she was too hungover to leave, and when she refused to drive me to school. She told the office that I was still too sick to attend.

Sadie's number was written on a slip of paper no bigger than the ones put into little fortune cookies, but by the end of that week, it felt like it weighed one hundred pounds.

Still, I didn't call.

I began to see entire scenes and dramas in the ceiling. In one of them, a cartoon bunny was running from a hunter, but they both ended up squished by a boulder in the end.

***

As Sadie's phone number became heavier and heavier in my pocket, my hatred for the popcorn ceiling grew as well. I found myself staring at it whenever I was in a foul mood. It always made things worse, but it was a sort of destructive pattern I'd gotten into.

The day when we got out of school at 1:00 p.m. for teacher training, and our parents were supposed to pick us up, my mother forgot to get me. Instead of waiting two hours for her to pick me up, I trudged home on foot. When I got home, sore and exhausted, at 2:30, I called the lab from the house phone and left a message telling my mother not to bother picking me up because I was already home.

I flopped on my back in my bedroom, right on the floor, and gave the popcorn ceiling a good look. I was planning to let myself be drawn into the grotesque assortment of faces and letting the shapes swirl and swallow me. I began to fall into a dizzy sort of detachment like usual until I noticed something. Since I studied the ceiling every day, I knew the bumps and shapes like the back of my hand. I knew exactly what I saw.

I saw new popcorn pieces.

My heart pounded in my chest. I stared at the new pieces in horror, considering that I might be hallucinating or seeing double. But no matter how long I stared, the new pieces stayed. And there were a lot of them.

I was waiting at the door when my mother came through. She looked slightly surprised to see me eagerly awaiting her, but she only widened her eyes for a moment before continuing for the liquor cabinet.

"Something wrong, Alfie?" She asked in a light tone.

"Have you redecorated in my room?" I breathed.

She gave me a sarcastic sort of look. "Not that I recall." She took a bottle of whiskey off the shelf. "Why?"

I spoke quickly, knowing my time with her sober self was limited.

"There are more popcorn pieces on the ceiling than there was yesterday."

She groaned, rolling her eyes and slamming the bottle on the counter.

"Alfie, I am very aware that you hate your room and especially hate that popcorn ceiling, but I am really too exhausted to deal with these little problems right now. I've been dealing with big problems all day. Problems that affect entire species of creatures."

"It's not about not liking it. There are more of them now. And there shouldn't be!"

Her voice became monotone, and I knew my time was up. She'd detached herself from the world prematurely. Still sober, but just as useless to me now as she would be an hour from now. "I think there's a hot dog or two in the fridge, so just take care of yourself tonight, k? I'm going to bed."

"But mom—"

Her eyes flashed fire for an instant.

My eyes didn't flash fire back at her, but I felt a lump of coal smoldering in the pit of my stomach.

"I had to walk all the way home. You forgot to pick me up. You didn't even ask how I got home!"

This rattled her.

"Well, I assumed you rode home with a friend. You called me at the lab to say not to worry about it."

"Yeah. The teachers told us we'd be getting out early so they could have meetings today. They've warned us every week for a month now and I gave you the paper every time!"

"Well," she said, putting a hand to her head. For a minute, I thought she might cry, which would have been a welcome sign that she cared. "This isn't my fault. I didn't know you were getting out early, and I thought you went home with a friend, that's all."

"I don't have friends!" I screamed at her. "Everyone thinks I'm weird, and the only friend I had gave me one cigarette so you banned him, too!"

"Oh, that's rich, Alfred. I'm trying to protect you from bad influences and now I'm the bad guy, right? I have sacrificed everything for you. Just because I'm not the kind of stay-at-home perfect mom you want doesn't mean I'm a bad mom."

"I don't need perfect. All I ever wanted was for you to act like you care."

She slumped a little and rubbed her eyes like was past her bedtime. "I know I can't ask a kid like you to understand but being an adult—being a parent—is really, really hard. Especially with your father gone."

"You know what's hard? Having a mom like you. I didn't ask to be your kid, you know."

There was a pause. Half a breath of space when I still held a shred of hope that my mother loved me, despite it all. If she had said something other than what she said next, I would have continued as we had before, taking whatever she dished out and cleaning up the mess after.

But she did say it. She said, "I didn't ask to be your mother."

I couldn't breathe for an instant, and when I did finally breathe again, the sound of my own insignificance rattled in my chest like a bad case of pneumonia. It was then that Sadie's phone number finally became too heavy to carry any longer, and I resolved to call her after my mother went to bed. When I heard the sounds of my mother snoring from somewhere within her bedroom (not likely in the bed, I knew, since she usually passed out drunk before she made it there), I crept to the kitchen and picked up the yellow phone. The curly cord was cool in my hand, just like Sadie's fingers had been when she'd given me the phone number. I paused, took a shaky breath, and dialed.

There were four rings, and then a muffled scraping of plastic as the receiver was picked up.

"Hello?" asked a delicate voice.

My body seized with fear and revulsion at what I'd dared to do. My knuckles gripped the phone until they turned white.

"Hello?" she asked again, more concern in her voice this time.

I flung the phone back toward its base but missed. It banged against the wall once, then bounced on its cord. I checked the hallway for signs of my mother, my heart jumping up and down my throat. I heard a raspy grumble come from down the hall, and I whimpered, not wanting to know what she'd do if she found out what I'd done. But she quieted again.

I grasped the phone in both hands, then placed it carefully back on the base. I slid to the floor and cried so hard I thought I might throw up.

When I was strong enough to pick myself up off the kitchen floor, I grabbed a lighter and returned to my room. My mom had found one cigarette in my backpack, but she didn't realize that my friend had been handing them to me for weeks. I had an entire pack's worth hidden, unused, in a box where I kept some extra baseball cards under my bed.

After everything that had happened, I resolved to do whatever I wanted from now on. I lit a cigarette and laid on my back in my bed, taking a long drag. I coughed and sputtered so violently that I dropped the cigarette on the carpet.

Once I'd caught my breath, I leaned over the side of the bed, about to grab the cigarette again. Before my fingers touched it, I felt a drop of something wet splatter on my cheek. I jumped, and my first reaction was to wipe it away before even looking to see what it was. My eyes slid up to the ceiling in slow motion because I was reluctant to see what was waiting for me.

I didn't see anything, but I heard a popping sound. Then one little dark thing dropped from one of the blobs of the popcorn ceiling. A slimy spot of brownish-green goo was left where it had been. A baby carpenter spider now stared at me as it sat on the lime green shag carpet. I looked at it, but I didn't move, hoping it wouldn't be attracted to me if I was still. I heard another pop.

I wasn't strong enough to play the statue game any longer as the truth came raining down on me eight furry legs at a time: the new popcorn globules I'd noticed were egg sacs. The popcorn ceiling became true to its name, my room a giant bag with pops every few seconds as the spiders fell to the shag carpet. I screamed and thrashed, swiping at them wildly to get them out of my hair and off my face. I danced and flailed with a madness I'd never felt before. I would have dashed my head open rather than let those spiders touch me.

I felt an excruciating pain at my ear and shot my hand up, grasping a hairy little ball of legs as it bit off a chunk of my ear and sliced in again, ready to take another piece. I ripped the spider off and gripped it so hard that it imploded in my hand into nothing but legs and goo.

I screamed as a wall of spiders surrounded me, writhing and climbing on top of each other in their haste. There were hundreds of them. Their scuttling sounded like the dry, amplified rasping of very fine sandpaper across human teeth. I grabbed a pillow from my bed and slammed it into them, turning in circles and whirling around to protect my sides.

"Get away!" I shouted at them.

That was when my mother burst through my door, her eyes red and annoyed-looking for just a millisecond before she saw the army of arachnids surrounding me. At her entrance, the spiders surged up and appeared to look back at her.

I felt heat at my back and whirled to see a low wall of flames behind me where I'd dropped the cigarette just moments before.

I looked at my mother and I silently prayed that she'd finally listen to me, just this once.

"Run!" I screeched.

Instead, she froze, wavering drunkenly from her whiskey binge. Then she took one faltering step backward, tripped, and tumbled down.

The spiders were drawn to the vibration of her fall, fleeing my area and swallowing her in their dark cloud. She was completely absorbed, and, at first, stunned to muteness. But then, she screamed, putting her hands out wide and flailing. She stood and spun in a jerky, faltering way, sending spiders flying across the room like missiles. She moaned and gurgled as the spiders bit every inch of her.

She became something that wasn't my mother, a writhing mass of black bodies coalescing in the shape of a human. Something that was a grotesque caricature—a spider-shadow, or a squirming black shell—of my mother stood its ground across the room, making clacking and skittering noises. Between the bloated spider bodies, her own skin made brief appearances and sudden disappearances, bloody and oozing.

She opened her mouth to scream, only to be silenced by a wave of spiders that jumped for the chance to get into her mouth and continue their biting from inside. Not long after their entrance, she went completely silent and limp. My mother collapsed into a heap, completely disappearing into the hill of spiders. Then her right eyeball escaped its socket, rolling like a marble and coming to a stop just a foot from me, the attention of the dark brown iris that I'd always so craved now pierced me squarely and intensely. For the first time, she was forced to look at nothing but me.

And when I saw that, death by fire seemed a better fate. I ran through the flames, opened the window, and jumped. I watched that house burn, and I also saw them streaming out, escaping: the spiders. Hundreds upon hundreds of them fleeing the flames. They could be anywhere now, breeding and adapting. They could be dormant, biding their time to breed, to lay their eggs, and fall on some unsuspecting victim in their sleep.

All I know is that when I am grown, I will only buy homes with smooth ceilings.

***

Note: This story was originally published on Kindle Vella.

5

Applied Arts

I arrived at the university, my tote bag digging a red trench into the soft flesh of my shoulder, shaking at the prospect of meeting my new roommate. It was early on a Saturday morning, and after trading tearful goodbyes with my parents, I was whisked away by a mob of attractive, peppy upperclassmen wearing matching *Peer Leader* t-shirts. In the warmth of the morning sun, they formed a semicircle and dazzled me with their healthful smiles and sun-kissed cheeks. They asked me my name, and I gave it. They asked me my major, and I gave that a little less easily. I lowered my eyes and admitted that I was one of the *Undecided.*

"Welcome, Maya! You belong here!" they all shouted. They whooped and pumped their fists. "Undecided rebel!"

Any shame I'd had over my lack of direction was lost when two of the guys picked me up and carried me on their shoulders in the middle of the group. I giggled and looked around the square at half a dozen other groups carrying freshmen like me to their dorms. I surveyed the tidy campus from on high, relishing the feeling of the sun on my skin. I just knew that it was only a matter of time before I'd become like these well-adjusted Peer Leaders.

When we arrived before the double doors of the Brentleywood dorm, I was placed briskly on the ground. My luggage was removed from the cart and divided among them. One of the girls began to whisper into her phone, her smile replaced by a face tightened with annoyance.

"I have to go," she hissed as she hung up. She turned to me, her white teeth smiling again. "Sorry, that's my boyfriend. Soon to be ex-boyfriend, I think, if he doesn't stop being so needy!"

"Well, love the one you're with I guess," I said.

She eyed one of the athletic guys who'd carried me, "I say that there are plenty of fish in the sea."

I thought to myself that it seemed like she wasn't trying hard enough to hold on to the fish she had, but I just smiled.

Just then, there was a shriek, and one of the Peer Leaders veered off in a zig-zag run. She waved her arms and spun in a circle. Her eyes were squeezed tight.

"Wasps," one of the Peer Leaders explained. "They send exterminators, but the wasps love the roof and always come back."

"That's why we stick freshmen here," a guy joked. They all laughed then, patted me on the back, and went on to the next freshman. I walked through the wide hallway of doors, looking for suite 102. When I arrived, I took a deep breath at the threshold and prepared myself to meet my new roommate.

But instead of a meeting, I was rewarded only by a drive-by sighting. I saw a wedge of short, brown hair emerge through the bathroom door on a body that was slim and tall. But before I could stutter, "Hi, I'm Maya! I'm your new roommate—" she'd rolled her baggage cart into one of the bedrooms and slammed the door.

I pulled a paper from my pocket and studied again the email that told me my new roommate's name and major. *Coral Thompson, Applied Arts*. My first thought was that maybe she was one of those who thought misery and isolation were requirements to be an artist. I bit my lip, folding the paper carefully and putting it on the plain oak desk in my bedroom. I *would* make friends with Coral Thompson, even if she was the melancholy type. I just had to get her out of her shell.

At that moment, I heard a knock, but before I was halfway across the room, the door swung wide to reveal a young woman with short pink hair. I smiled despite myself, in the involuntary manner in which a person might find themselves smiling at a cute dog or a baby. You couldn't help but smile in her presence. She strode into the room on rainbow socks in red converse shoes and extended her hand.

"I'm Malorie, the hall leader. Or, as others call me, hall *mom*. You can call me Mal. I'm the one who makes sure we only do misdemeanor-level stupid around here and that nobody drinks themselves to death."

"Maya," I said, grinning. "Love your socks."

"Thanks! I'm rounding up everybody for brunch at the dining hall for a little get-to-know-you time," Mal said. "Are you free?"

I considered Mal with her swingy pink hair and her bright socks, and then I looked at the door that separated me from Coral. My smile faded as I felt the weight of that heavy door.

"Thanks, Mal. I think I'd like to go next time but, you know, I want to get to know my roommate a little better."

Mal looked at the door now and frowned. "Oh! Your roomie's here? Of course, you should bring them too! We're leaving in ten."

I brightened again. "Okay. See you there!"

"Catch ya later, babes."

I laughed at this—nobody'd ever called me *babes* before. My cheeks flushed as I was flooded with optimism again. I went straight to Coral's room and knocked on the door.

I listened to the sounds on the other side. There was shuffling and shifting, and maybe humming, but she didn't open. My heart began to beat fast even though I knew it was silly to feel nervous. I knocked louder.

"Busy," came through the door like a growl.

I didn't go to the dorm brunch. The arrival, the unpacking, the new people...it all seemed overwhelming after my roommate's rejection. I went to my room and took a long nap.

***

By the end of that first semester, I'd studied calculus, geography, writing 101, and enough loneliness to count as an actual extracurricular.

I'd created a game for myself at night when the multistory dormitories became a checkerboard of light and dark squares. I counted the yellow windows, the ones that indicated the presence of their inhabitants. Alone in my bed, I'd count the other losers. Kids who weren't partying or in clubs either. Kids who were sitting in their rooms alone just like me. It gave me some comfort to peer into the yellow and see that some nameless chick was watching Gray's Anatomy alone again, or that the dude on the 3rd floor across the way was drowning his loneliness in chips and video games. *I'm not the only one*, I'd tell myself. *There are others.*

Every day with Coral as a roommate was like living with a ghost. We lived within yards of each other but hardly ever made contact. By the end of the first month, I became convinced that she'd been studying my patterns and was avoiding me on purpose. I tried lingering in the living area, flipping through magazines and watching television to pass the time, hoping to catch her on her way in or out. But somehow, she was always so fast or so involved in a conversation on the phone that there was never a chance to say a word to her before she slipped by behind the solid barricade of the oak door.

One day, as she sped past on her way to the shower, I happened to notice that she suffered from what seemed to be a severe case of acne. All over her face, neck, and arms were red, inflamed dots that made her otherwise pretty face look disfigured. I thought that maybe her self-consciousness about the blemishes was making her reclusive.

Still, by the end of the second month, I began to wonder what was so wrong about *me* that I should be shunned like that. And by the end of the semester, I accepted it as what I deserved. My invisibility to Coral became a part of me, like a second skin. I began to imagine that the way Coral saw me was the way everyone saw me.

Mal still came by every so often with her bright hair, which had been changed to teal by mid-semester, and her even brighter outlook. She offered me invitations almost daily to dorm events, to lunch with her, and to try out various clubs. But soon, I found myself avoiding her in the same way that Coral avoided me. I felt so rejected, so overwhelmed by my failure to make friends with my roommate that I couldn't stand Mal's happy, well-balanced outlook. Her rainbow clothes made me sick. Sometimes, when she came to my room late in the evening "just to check" on me, I thought I saw a flicker of pity in her eyes, and that made it even worse. I found myself coming out of my room almost as infrequently as Coral.

I got so depressed that I think it would have killed me, had something else not tried to kill me first.

***

Mal had busted into my suite without knocking that day. I gaped at her and quickly slurped up the ramen noodles dangling from my lips.

"You've not come out in days. What's going on?" She demanded.

"I'm just, you know, hanging out."

"You're not hanging out. You're wallowing. I'm worried about you."

I stared at the butterfly clips in her teal hair. One was yellow, the other orange.

"Come out to dinner with us. Otherwise, I'm going to the school therapist myself and making an appointment for you."

I groaned. "I'm fine. Really. Some people just don't feel the need to go out all the time, you know. I'm an introvert." I knew as I said it that it was a lie. Memories flooded back of my large group of high school friends, the laughter, my raucous personality. I was faded now, a black-and-white copy walking around in the world where my old self had been.

Mal's knuckles went white as she gripped the door. "I just wish you'd come out just *once*," she said. "Please."

I wasn't sure, but I thought I saw a small pool growing in the whites of her eyes.

A stone had lodged itself in my throat and I couldn't speak.

She turned away. "Take care of yourself."

After she left, I did go out. I went out to the liquor store and brought back orange juice and vodka. I'd only had one or two illicit drinks at high school parties in the past, so I had no idea what effect the hard alcohol would have on me.

Three drinks in, I began to get my self-confidence back. I heard a few thumps from Coral's room and turned my head to glare at the old oak door. She was in there. Ignoring me.

Again.

Who did she think she was, acting like I didn't exist? I could be a good roommate if she let me. Funny. Smart. Loyal. I have a lot of good qualities. My thoughts were a slurry of all the outrage and doubt of the whole semester.

I wobbled up off the couch and lurched toward Coral's door. I was going to go in there and *make* her talk to me. The vodka had warmed my face and awakened my courage. My sweaty hand slipped off the door once, but on the second try, I grabbed it and swung the door open. I felt the room spin as I stumbled into Coral's room. I'd never actually seen it before, and now I was seeing it drunk.

I struggled to understand what my drunken eyes were telling me they saw. There were things you'd expect in an art major's room: charcoal pencils scattered about, papers and sketches haphazardly covering every surface, and jugs of paints and glues leaning against bookshelves.

But the thing in the corner by the window did not belong.

The window was draped with a dark curtain, but I could see that it was open and letting in little puffs of wind. Wind, and with it, *wasps.*

Wasps filed in and out of her room in a businesslike way, attending to their home and leaving again. Their *home* was the thing in the corner that did not belong.

The wasps' home was a face. It was humanoid, with high cheekbones coated in the khaki-looking color of the wasp's nest, with eyes agape and mouth yawning wide. Wasps crawled in and out of the eye sockets, through the nose and ears, and skittered out of the dark mouth. Around the head were more nests. Smaller ones. Together, a giant heap of wasp nests, where the insects hummed and thrummed within.

I swallowed hard as I looked at the face and realized that it wasn't a true wasp's nest, but rather something made out of plaster and adopted by the insects. The likeness, the face, looked exactly like my own. My cheekbones, my full lips, and my curly hair. But it had been twisted, formed into an expression of pain and torture. I touched my face and stumbled back.

"Get out!" Coral screeched. "It's not ready yet," she moaned, holding her head in her hands like it might explode.

Before I knew what to do, she grabbed me. Her ragged, short fingernails raked my arms and left spotted trails of blood. Awakened from my daze by the pain, I felt a surge of courage and clawed right back.

We tumbled to the ground and she scratched more—this time at my face. I swatted at her hands as she dragged her nails down my cheeks and eyelids. She pulled my hair.

"I'm going to get you expelled! Arrested!" I screamed at her as I felt a chunk of my hair come away in her fist. "What the Hell is this?"

She grabbed me around the neck and squeezed. "It's art," she hissed against my ear. I looked up at the ceiling and noticed that her room was covered in brown squares. *Sound-proofing.* If I was going to survive, it had to be by my own hands. Nobody could hear me.

I headbutted her. She crumpled, and I shoved her off me. I looked at the nest. The buzzing grew stronger and more urgent. The sound surged like a wave as a cluster of wasps charged and attacked my hand. I watched them in something like a trance. I felt their first stings, sharp and burning, and I was brought back into senses and then out again with wild fear. Sweat dripped into my eyes, blurring my vision. I could see more wasps were making their way out of the human-head-shaped blob of a nest. I swatted the first wasps off and stumbled back.

And when I swatted one, it flew into my nose.

Even though I knew there were hundreds of other wasps coming for me, my world had now been reduced to the size of my nose, where the angry wasp was stinging and crawling and buzzing and refusing to come out. I tilted my head and shook it wildly, screaming, shaking my limbs, jerking with each new sting. I was a mad puppet driven by an insect. My screams were childlike yelps, sharp and staccato. Wasps coated my limbs, but it was nothing compared to the horror of the one exploring my face from the inside.

"Help me!" I screeched, as if Coral would. As I flailed blindly, I fell into the nest and heard it crunch.

"It's ruined!" Coral cried.

"Help," I wailed. The wasps were now a mask over my face. I breathed in and they were in my mouth, skittering and stinging and beating their wings. I spat and choked them out, except for one that remained and stung down my throat until I swallowed it whole. My throat swelled and I wheezed, but they kept coming. The one in my nose continued to sting until the nostril was completely blocked off. My entire body began to surge with the waves of pain in my body and my terror swelled with each new buzz and sting. My skin boiled and blistered and split. Breathing was nearly impossible.

Soon, I couldn't even scream. I couldn't see. The wasps had stung everything, removing all my senses except for my ability to feel pain. I rolled around, weakly swatting whatever I could reach, but it was useless. Right before I passed out, I heard the sound of Carol's feet retreating and the door being slammed shut. It was oblivion that I hoped for. At least there wouldn't be wasps there.

***

When I woke up, there were tubes in my arm and coming out of my nose. A hospital bed, instead of oblivion, greeted me. That, and Mal.

"Maya!" She shouted. She gathered me into a strong hug, sending waves of pain down through my ruined skin.

"Ow," I moaned.

"Sorry!" She said, biting her lip. "Oh, I'm so sorry. I wasn't thinking. Maya, I'm so sorry. This is all my fault. I'm the worst hall leader. I can't believe there were wasp nests on my floor and I didn't even know."

I coughed, and pain exploded in my throat. "Brunch?" I finally rasped.

Her face twisted in confusion. Then, she wiped her eyes and laughed. "As soon as you're out. Yes, you can have all the brunch you want. I'm *never* letting you skip brunch again."

I nodded, smiling while knowing that it must look like a grotesque approximation.

"And to think, all this time," Mal continued, "I thought maybe you just didn't like me!"

6

Black Butterfly

The Ross family's new home was not right.

To Rosalin Ross, who'd recently been demoted to the role of the invisible older sibling, relaxing at the new house was as hopeless as relaxing in a hornet's nest. During the day, movers and repairmen filed in and out the front door, and during the night, her baby brother Marcus screamed without end.

As far as Rosalin was concerned, there was no reason for all these changes. Their lives had been perfect in the city. There was no reason for them to move to this rural wooded area, and to a tiny school where she would be an outsider. There was no reason for them to have added squirmy, screaming Marcus to their family. They'd been happy before.

Marcus' birth had felt like a betrayal, as if she hadn't been enough for her parents. It was the only explanation she could think of for why they'd do such a thing. Then, when they'd announced the move shortly after, she'd been even more angry, sure that her parents were trying to ruin her life on purpose.

Rosalin kicked over one of the cardboard boxes stacked in her room. A stack of winter sweaters spilled out on the floor. As she knelt to pick one up, she heard a scuffling in the hall that meant Marcus was coming.

Marcus paused at the threshold to her room and gave her a big oblivious grin.

"Get out," Rosalin warned. She waved him away.

Mother's silhouette appeared behind Marcus in the door. "Be nice."

"Get out, please," Rosalin sneered, sticking out her tongue.

Marcus continued to invade and was about to destroy a notebook before Mother scooped him up and sat on the bed.

"I don't understand, Rosalin. This isn't like you to be so unkind. Why won't you play with Marcus?"

Rosalin scowled. She wanted to say a lot of things. For one, she was sick of Marcus crying all night. She was sick of her parents only giving her attention when she'd done something wrong. She felt confused because, even though their family was bigger than ever, she'd never felt so alone. But Rosalin didn't know how to put this into words that her mother would understand. Tears came to her eyes.

"Because he just ruins everything," she muttered.

"I know Marcus can't do a lot right now, but when he gets older, you two can have fun together. But part of being a family is doing things for one another even though we might not get anything in return."

Mother launched into a long speech about family as Marcus continued to crawl all over her. Rosalin turned to the window and watched the pine trees sway in the breeze.

All at once, a huge black butterfly landed on the window. It wasn't a dull black—it was an iridescent color that glinted in the light like the rainbow film on an oil slick or the shimmer on a raven's wing. At the bottom wingtips, a lacy white edge flared out like a petticoat. The wingspan was at least the size of two adult hands put together. The beautiful wings flapped once, very slowly, as if showing off its rainbow luster, and then it flew away.

Rosalin hopped to her feet at once. "Did you see that?" she shouted.

"Rosalin, were you even listening?"

"There was a huge black butterfly right there on the window!"

Her mother stood and her face tightened with anger. "Young lady, I don't care if you saw a unicorn. When I'm speaking, I would appreciate being listened to. Nobody ever listens..." her voice trailed off. Her mother's eyes looked suddenly wet.

Rosalin's cheeks flushed pink and she looked at the floor.

"Nevermind," Mother sighed. She put Marcus on her hip as she left and clicked the door shut.

The next morning, Rosalin happened to look out the window as she got ready for school. In the middle of the backyard, she caught a glimpse of the black butterfly bobbing up and down with the breeze. She blinked only once, and when she opened her eyes, the butterfly was gone. Then, on the drive to school, she saw it again. It smacked into the windshield, flapped wildly, and dissolved before her eyes. When she screamed, her mother yelled that Rosalin had almost caused a wreck. Her mother hadn't seen it.

That night, Rosalin waited in the backyard until the butterfly finally emerged from a rose bush. It floated right toward her. The natural response was to hold out her finger to see if it would land.
It landed on the tip of her index finger.

The world turned gray. The house disappeared, the backyard became a wild overgrowth, and everything around took on a blue-gray cast, as if someone had put a moody photo filter over the whole world. Before her eyes, the black butterfly transformed into a girl that was like an exact copy of Rosalin but with strange eyes that were solid black from lid to center. A thick blue mist skirted around her twin's ankles.

"What are you?" Rosalin said.

The creature tilted its head. Its voice sounded like Rosalin's but airier and with a monotone quality. The voice reminded her of the steadily spinning threads in her mother's sewing machine: mechanical and smooth.

"We are the fae," her twin said.

"A fairy?" Rosalin asked.

The creature didn't answer. Instead, it bowed and presented Rosalin with a crown of white roses. As if this were a signal, dozens of faeries now emerged from behind the gnarled trees. The faeries had closed-mouth, wide smiles as they put the crown on her head.

"All hail queen Rosalin!" they chanted.

Rosalin beamed. They took her to a pavilion decorated with bright streamers and danced to beautiful music that seemed to boom directly from the great gray sky. A feast of strange, red fruits and tiny cakes had been laid out on a long table. Rosalin ate to bursting. Finally, her twin faerie offered her hand, and when Rosalin took it, she was home. Nobody had even noticed she'd gone.

Rosalin spent the entire next day waiting to see the black butterfly again. In the evening, she finally spied it weaving through the limbs of a pine tree in the backyard. But on her way out the door, she almost tripped over Marcus. She looked down to say something snarky but noticed that he seemed to be holding something quite small.

He gave her a dimpled smile and said, "Lin."

Rosalin felt a connection to him with a suddenness that hurt like a surprise pinprick. "Did you just try to say my name?"

"Lin!" he said, giggling. He reached out and she picked him up.

"Mom!" Rosalin yelled. "He just said my name!"

Her mother had been sitting on the couch, and she jumped up. "Oh my gosh! Did I hear you right? He said your name?"

For a moment, everyone smiled.

Rosalin opened Marcus' palm and took an iron nail away. "Oh no! You can't have that!"

She showed the nail to her mother. "Maybe a repairman dropped it."

"Thank goodness you found this. He could have choked! What a good big sister you are," her mother said, touching Rosalin's shoulder. "I always knew you would be."

Rosalin felt a warm glow inside. But then, she also felt the pull of the black butterfly waiting for her in the backyard.

"I'm going out to play," she said.

When she arrived, she could feel something different in the faerie realm. There was a stillness over the gray land, a feeling of anticipation.

The faerie appeared as before, but this time she looked grim. Maybe even a little angry.

"You can't come here anymore unless you bring the baby. If you bring him, you'll be our queen."

"My brother? Why do you want him?"

For the first time, the faerie revealed her teeth: piranha-like and yellow.

Rosalin recoiled. She didn't want those teeth anywhere near Marcus.

"We only come when we're summoned," the faerie said in her spider-silk voice.

"I didn't summon you!"

The creature's eyes flashed from black to red. "You didn't wish for your little brother to disappear?"

"I didn't mean it."

"You did," she hissed.

Rosalin backed away. "No. Take me home right now."

"If we can't have him, we will have *you*!" The faerie screeched. Sharp claws burst from her fingertips. She pounced.

Still holding the iron nail she'd taken from Marcus, Rosalin slashed out and pricked the faerie's palm. When the nail touched the faerie, everything dissipated. The faerie twin and her terrifying teeth were gone.

Rosalin ran into the house. She slammed the door. Locked it. She dashed to Marcus, gathering him in a hug.

"I'm sorry," she whispered against his bald head.

Their mother crossed the room and, seeing her children hugging, froze in her tracks. She placed her hand on her heart, smiling.

The faeries never had a reason to visit again.

***

Note: This story was first published in Mother Ghost's Grimm Volume 1.

7

Edgar Falls Run

Nora and I were the only ones in the Edgar Falls Salon and Spa this time of night—a special late-night appointment we'd reserved to accommodate Nora's work schedule as a nurse at the local hospital. We sat in oversized faux-leather chairs with our feet in warm, bubbling water. The single esthetician alternated between our feet in a slow, tired-looking dance.

"A fat high school basketball coach," I said, rubbing my bad leg. "Who ever heard of that? I'm a joke."

"Hey, you're not just a fat high school basketball coach," Nora replied in an upbeat tone, "You're a fat P.E. teacher, too." She shot me an impish grin.

I laughed, appreciating the fact that my friend didn't try to lie to me to make me feel better. I always could trust Nora.

I twirled my feet around in the bubbling water for the foot bath below me. I wrinkled my nose as a strong whiff of peppermint met my nose. Whoever decided that feet were supposed to smell minty? It's not like they were going into anyone's mouth. This was my first pedicure, and I found the entire ritual ridiculous and beyond pointless.

I'd invited Nora because we hadn't spoken in months, and it was the first thing that came to my mind to do that sounded like something normal women do together.

The previous evening, I'd been doing one of my nightly grocery store runs for comfort food when my cart ran into something hard with a metallic clang. The force sent my midsection right into the cart's handlebar and the liters of soda and tubs of ice cream tumbling around crazily inside the cart.

"Oof!" I'd said, and I was already thinking about the curse words I wanted to use on whoever'd been rude enough to exit an aisle without looking first.

I looked up from my cart, my first thought annoyance that now I'd have to wait even longer before opening my sodas so they wouldn't explode, and I opened my mouth to let the offender have a piece of my mind.

But when I lifted my eyes, I saw Nora, my best friend. Or, rather, my *former* best friend. Before I'd gone MIA and pushed her out of my life.

"Kayla?" She said, her irritated expression morphing into recognition. She shifted her weight with an awkward movement of her legs and flitted her eyes away from me, toward a stack of canned corn. "How have you been?"

"Oh, fine," I said, as I always did when people asked that question. Nobody actually wanted the answer when you were chronically depressed.

Our conversation continued at a slow hobble, but it was an important meeting. I'd been afraid to let Nora see me like this: Fat, depressed, and boring. I'd avoided her ever since the traumatic ACL repair surgery that had left me this way. I had been conveniently missing her calls for months and replying with excuses to her invitations to hang out. At the end of our chat in the grocery aisle, she started to roll away, and I felt something catch in my throat.

"Nora!" I'd said, my heard thudding against my rib cage.

Her cart's wheels squeaked to a halt.

"Want to hang out tomorrow?" I was afraid she would give me a verbal slap to the face to punish me for my months of avoidance.

Instead she gave me a small, knowing smile. "Sure, Kay. Just tell me when and where."

Panicked, I thought of the first thing that came to mind.

So now we were getting our feet buffed and our nails painted, even though neither of us really cared for that sort of thing.

We had always been rough-and-tumble girls, and our friendship had been predicated on shared experiences of running, climbing, and thrill-seeking. Now that I didn't do those things anymore, it had seemed like there wasn't any reason to hang out.

As I looked at my feet, I couldn't help but notice Nora's thin, toned calves out of the corner of my eye. By contrast, my own legs looked bloated and disgusting. I lifted my leg in the air and let my foot come down hard, making a splash that hit Nora's legs.

She laughed. "Kayla, it's temporary. You'll snap out of this, as soon as your leg is healed up." Nora said. She yelped as the esthetician prodded her cuticles. "Easy on that toe, sister!" she said, looking down.

"Yeah, when it's healed..." I said, my speech trailing off. I hadn't admitted yet that my doctor had cleared me for regular physical activity months ago. Every time I wanted to run, either in my students' gym class, at basketball games, or on my own time, my legs felt paralyzed, as if I'd forgotten how to move them. I wanted to run, but I couldn't. It seemed like that part of my life was over now.

It was too much to admit to my longtime friend. I'd been the one who had taken a gap year to go backpacking across Europe. I couch surfed regularly when I wanted to travel across state lines, not always making plans ahead of time. My hair, which was sporting a several inches of dark roots, held evidence of pink color at the ends. In the past I'd sported pixie cuts and other wild styles. I'd even buzzed my head once just to see what it would look like.

I hadn't ever been afraid of anything like this before.

I needed a way to change the subject, so I snatched the newspaper from the small square table that sat between our chairs. I rifled through the pages until one of the headlines caught my eye.

EDGAR FALLS WOMEN GO MISSING

"Have you heard about the Edgar Falls disappearances?" I asked. "Wild stuff. Nothing like this ever happens here. Gives me the creeps." And another good reason not to pick running back up again.

Nora scoffed. "Yeah, for a few months there I thought *you* were one of the disappeared women."

"Ha. Ha," I said. "Not like I was recovering from surgery or anything."

"You've been 'recovering' for almost a year now," Nora said. She glared at me for a moment, but then her expression softened. "Was the recovery too bad? For the surgery?"

I felt tears stinging my eyes at the casual way she brought it up, as if we were discussing the weather. *How are the roads today? Is there much rain?* I pretended to cough to choke down the sob that wanted to come out.

To say that the subject of the surgery was a trigger would be an understatement. The subject of the surgery was a landmine.

My mind raced with anxiety and regret. I had known that meeting up with Nora would be a mistake. I wasn't ready to rejoin the regular world yet. I felt my heart rate increase and my breathing became shallow and fast.

"Nothing worth talking about," I managed to say in what I hoped was a casual tone.

My heart continued to pound. I opened my phone and angled it away from Nora so she couldn't see what I was doing. I went into my phone settings and played the notification sound to make it seem like I'd received a text message.

"Oh man," I said. I performed a frustrated-sounding sigh.

"What? Is that Corwin? Tell him you're busy," Nora said, giving me a playful warning glance. "This is girl time."

I winced at the mention of my old boyfriend. Had it been that long since Nora and I had hung out? Did she really not know that he was gone from my life? I didn't want to correct her and get into that story on top of the panic I was already feeling.

"No...It's my mom. Kipper got out of the fence and she can't find him anywhere," I lied. "She thinks he might come back if he hears my voice. I've got to go. I love that little pain in the butt." I looked at the esthetician, who was currently rubbing a peach-scented exfoliating scrub over my heels.

"Can I get a towel?" I asked her. "I'm going to need to get out here."

"But you paid for a paraffin dip," the woman said, frozen mid-scrub.

"It's okay. Just keep the extra," I said, trying to keep the nervousness from creeping into my voice.

"Well, I guess I'm going to get out of here too, then," Nora said to her in a clipped voice, not even attempting to conceal her irritation.

"Sorry, Nor. I just have to do this."

"Ugh. He's a farm dog, isn't he? What kind of trouble could he get into? I bet he'll be back in time for dinner," Nora said.

I looked at her for a moment and considered coming clean about what was wrong. Her eyebrows were pressed together in a silent plea. She missed me. I was one of her closest friends, after all.

I wanted to tell her what had happened to me during my ACL surgery. Maybe I would find healing just saying the words out loud.

My mind took me back to that terrifying event as I struggled to find the words to describe what had happened during the surgery.

The fog had lifted from my mind even though my eyes were still closed. No, that was wrong. It wasn't like a fog lifted from my brain—it was as if a curtain had been ripped down and a blinding torrent of sensation had rushed in on me all at once.

The first sensation was pain. I felt like my entire left leg was on fire. I wanted to scream, but I found myself unable to move my vocal cords. I wanted to flinch away from the pressure and poking sensations I felt in and around my knee, but I couldn't move my muscles, either.

I was paralyzed and yet fully conscious.

I heard sounds: the beeping monitors, the clinking of metal tools on rolling trays, and someone clearing their throat. I heard the middle of a conversation.

"Looking forward to the weekend?" a disembodied female voice said.

"Yeah," replied another. "I'm going to the lake with Monty."

"That's great," the woman replied. "Hand me the gauze and that other scalpel, please?"

I tried to interject. To scream *I'm awake*, but all I couldn't even open my eyes or wiggle my toes to communicate.

I felt sharp tugging and intense pressure at my knee joint and I wondered how long the surgery would last. I didn't know if I could last much longer, because the pain was so intense. Yet, what other choice did I have? I couldn't move. I felt sweat pooling at my armpits and I smelled the coffee breath of the person standing near my head. The smell sent a wave of nausea through me, and for a moment I hoped that I might throw up so they would know that I was awake.

"What's going on with her heart rate?" The woman said.

"Shit!" I heard someone mutter in a panicked voice. "Daniel, have you been watching that BIS monitor?"

"Crap!" another voice replied. "She was fine a minute ago."

"Fix it!" the woman commanded. "God, it's like you're fresh from school. She might be aware."

Then it had all gone black again. The next thing I'd remembered was waking up in a blue-dotted hospital gown with a large bandage on my knee.

A fresh-faced nurse with a swinging yellow ponytail skipped into my room with a clipboard and a smile, shoving a chart with cartoon faces in my face.

"Rate your pain on a scale of one to ten, please," she chirped.

My mouth was dry as sandpaper as I swallowed and pointed to the number one. I felt no pain anymore, but the memories of my wakeful period were still vivid and intense.

I thought about telling her about what had happened, but what good would it have done? What could they do now?

So I didn't tell anyone.

"Earth to Kayla..." Nora said, bringing me back to the present moment.

The esthetician working on my feet stood, looking annoyed at the interruption in her regular routine.

Nora didn't know what I was hiding, but with the searching look she was giving me, I think she knew that something was up between us. She just didn't know what.

"I don't want to get blamed if something happens to Kipper," I said, avoiding Nora's eyes. "We should do this again," I added. I gave her my best fake smile.

Nora snorted in reply. She'd never been one to hide her opinions and feelings.

I hadn't either, until the surgery.

After I put on my sandals and stood, Nora grabbed my arm.

Despite the firmness of her grasp, her face softened as she spoke. "I know something has been up since the surgery. I don't know what it is. But...why don't we try to do something together like we used to?"

I felt a small amount of relief. She wasn't giving up on our friendship yet, even though I was acting like a complete weirdo. That was good, right?

"Yeah, we aren't really froo-froo girls, are we?" I said.

"Hmph," said the asthetician from the floor where she was cleaning up the foot tubs and manicure accessories.

"No offense," I said in the nail tech's direction. "I'll be honest—this was my first pedicure. It's not really my thing." I felt my heart rate decrease. The subject had changed away from the surgery, and soon I'd be home and safe from questions again.

"Why don't we go running again, Kayla? Tomorrow night. Just like we used to before you got injured."

All of the calmness that had been building inside me was rendered inert in an instant.

"I already told you. I can't run anymore."

"Bullshit," Nora said. Her voice was clipped and sharp and left no room for arguing.

"Okay. I...*won't* run anymore," I said. I sighed, looking at the nail tech who was now impatiently tapping a finger on the countertop by the register. "Can we finish this conversation outside?"

After we left the spa, we went to the parking lot. The sun had slipped under the horizon and the streetlamps came on. The lights buzzed, and one of them flickered on and off when we passed it. I felt my mood plunge as this happened, as if the world around me dimmed wherever I went. It had sure felt like that lately.

"I know I should be able to run," I admitted to Nora, my voice quiet. "It's just...I can't make my legs go. Like...It's hard to explain."

"Try me," she said.

As I gathered the words in my mind, I heard the wind whistle through the gap in the old wooden fence that surrounded the parking lot. The sound sent a shiver down my spine despite the warmth of the summer night.

"You ever feel have a word on the tip of your tongue? Like...you know that you know it, deep down, but some part of your brain just is blocking you so that you're helpless to remember it? And it's always a really stupid-easy word, too, right?"

"Yeah, all the time."

"Well, it's like that. Except with my legs. And running. My legs don't remember how to run."

"Hm. I'm still not sure that makes sense."

Just then, a rumbling pickup truck squealed as it turned into the parking lot. It slowed as it neared us, the bright headlights making it hard to see the driver until it idled directly in front of us.

For a moment, my heart stuck in my throat as it appeared that the truck was headed straight for us. I prepared my muscles to jump, but knew I probably wouldn't be able to make myself move in time.

Thankfully, the truck squealed to a stop mere feet away.

"You ladies should get home! Haven't you heard there's some loon out snatchin' women?" The man shouted at us from under a blue ball cap.

"Oh I'd like to see somebody try to nab me," Nora said with a mischievous grin. "How ya' doin', Abe?"

"Fine, just fine. But you won't be if you don't haul tail home. Git!"

"Thanks, Abe. Appreciate your concern. Truly," Nora said, her voice dripping with sarcasm.

"Yuns' better listen, or you'll be the next headline," he said, shaking his head.

Then he revved the old truck and sputtered out of the parking lot.

"Who's that?" I asked.

"My neighbor," Nora said. "He likes to think it's his job to make sure girls abide by curfew...even the ones in their thirties," she scoffed. "Small towns. You never really get to grow up in some peoples' eyes I guess."

"Yeah," I said, feeling wistful. "I'd had such high hopes of leaving someday, and yet after all my adventures, I ended up here anyway."

"Oh, put away that tiny violin," she said. "Now, stop changing the subject. What is this about you not remembering how to run?" She leaned back against her SUV.

"I guess I'm also," I released a heavy sigh, "like, scared shitless that as soon as I do, I'll tear my ACL again. Or experience that pain again. Or just that *something* will happen."

"There we have it," Nora said with a satisfied look on her face. She grabbed my shoulders and gave me a playful shake. "There. Now don't you feel better?"

"Yeah," I said, even though I felt worse to tell the truth. I felt my face burning with embarrassment.

"Well, if you don't think you can run, let's just start with baby steps. We can walk! There's no shame in that."

She was wrong about that. Me, a former women's college basketball player who got a full ride scholarship for my physical prowess, reduced to walking for exercise. But I had already been pushing Nora away for months, so I had to give her something.

"I think I can walk," I said with a reluctant expression that I hoped looked like a smile but felt more like a grimace.

"Atta girl!" She whooped and whirled her fist around in the air as if she were cheering on a football team. "We should go tomorrow night when I get off work and it's cool outside." She wiped at her brow which glistened with sweat under the streetlamps. "I swear, Edgar Falls is the frying pan of God in the summer."

"Okay. Tomorrow it is." This felt odd and unpracticed, making social plans. I used to go out all the time, and now planning a walk felt exhausting. I was just ready for it to be over and to sink into the comfort of my bed.

"8:00," she said, aiming another look of playful chastisement at me, "and if you find Kipper today, put him in a crate before we leave for our walk. No backing out."

"Yeah, yeah," I said, but I couldn't help but smile. Maybe things really could be normal again.

On my drive home, I felt exhausted from the effort of being social. I didn't used to be that way, but now more than a few minutes of talking with someone left me feeling drained. I was looking forward to eating whatever my mother had cooked for dinner and then traipsing upstairs to my comfortable bed.

Instead, my mother had planned a serious discussion.

I walked into the door to the smell of rosemary and roasted chicken, and I gave Kipper a pat. He wagged his tail and panted.

When I sat at the dinner table, I knew something was up when my mom put her fork down in a delicate motion and cleared her throat. She gave my father a significant glance and he did the same.

"Kayla, honey."

"What?"

"Your father and I love having you here, but we think maybe you'd be happier with a space of your own. You know, with some privacy for yourself." She smiled brightly.

Translation: *We're sick of having you freeload here.*

I swallowed, and the mashed potatoes that went down my throat felt like a hard lump of rocks all the way down.

"Yeah," I said, "just as soon as my leg is better."

I had moved back in with my parents after the surgery so they could help take care of me while I recovered. It was supposed to have been temporary. I knew that I'd overstayed my welcome, but I couldn't bring myself to go back to my empty apartment by myself. It scared me.

"It's just...Well, it's been a year, sweetheart."

"Gotta' pick yourself up by your bootstraps. Get back on the horse. Stand back up after you fall. Fall down seven times, stand up eight," my father said in an odd, strained tenor. His voice sounded strained, as if he realized he was drowning in clichés but was unable to stop himself. He'd always been terrible at this sort of thing. In a better mood, it would have made me laugh.

I answered them with silence.

My mom frowned at my dad and then looked back at me. Then she looked down at her plate and cut a thin slice of chicken. "Maybe you could move in with Corwin? You two have been dating for a long time...I'm sure he'd be happy to help you out while you recovered."

My silverware clattered as I dropped the fork and knife. My hands trembled with frustration, and I took a long swig from my wine glass, hoping the alcohol would quell my anger.

"There is no Corwin," I said darkly. How had my mother not realized that already? He hadn't been to the house in months.

"What happened?" My mother said. Bless her heart—she looked so concerned.

I took another large swig of my wine and coughed as some of the liquid went down my windpipe. How could I tell her? How could I explain to my mother, the woman who loved me more than anyone in the world, that my longtime boyfriend had left me at the first sign of adversity? When my moods darkened, he had started ending dates early. Eventually, he stopped asking me on them. And when my waistline and thighs had grown, well then he stopped coming on dates even when I'd asked *him*.

How could I tell her that I was a bad judge of character? That I'd dated someone vain and superficial? I didn't want to face that embarrassment.

"We broke up," I said. "It was months ago." And since there was nothing else to say, I stood from the table and went to bed.

The next day I avoided my parents, leaving the house for work even earlier than usually so I wouldn't accidentally bump into them.

At school, I had trouble keeping my eyes open, having slept very little the night before. I'd been thinking about what a mess I had made of my life. Most of all, I was thinking about how helpless I felt to change any of it. I yawned as I watched my gym class take place from a bench. The students were in the gym doing *free time*, because I was too tired to organize anything else. *Free time* meant they could go to one of the four corners of the gym and play either basketball, volleyball, dodge ball, or tag.

The big problem with free time days was that there would inevitably be a corner that took a rest break that turned into social time for the students. That was when I had to get up and prod them to move around and play again, otherwise there would be trouble. I'd waited too long to break the groups apart this time, and a small huddle of girls had gathered around someone in the dodge ball corner.

I groaned as I stood and lumbered over to the group of girls, feeling aggravated that they'd made me stand up from my comfortable spot on the bench.

The girls were chanting something, and as I got closer I was able to make the words out.

"Wendy the Weirdo! Wendy the Weirdo!"

Great, I thought, *now I have a bullying situation to deal with.*

As I approached the group, the girls parted, revealing Wendy, a thirteen-year-old social outcast who was often the subject of such bullying.

"This is unacceptable behavior!" I said, huffing from the effort of walking across the gym. "Girls, go to the locker room. Now. Think about what you've done until I come to talk to you."

Wendy wiped her eyes and started to stand up, but I put out a hand in the air to stop her from leaving.

"Wendy? Are you all right?" I felt bad for Wendy. Her family life was chaotic and she had no home to speak of. Instead, she was juggled from family member to family member, depending on who was the most stable at the time. It made her vulnerable, and the other students knew it.

"Yes, Miss Kayla."

"What happened?"

"I told them about the voices," she said, her vocal chords trembling. "What they've been saying. I wanted to warn them. We all need to be careful."

I gulped. I'd tried to refer Wendy before to a counselor for the voices she reported hearing, but nothing had helped yet.

"What are they saying, Wendy?" I had to ask, even though I knew it wasn't good to indulge her imagination.

"The possessions are starting again."

I felt a chill down my spine. Where had Wendy heard about the Edgar Falls murders of 1981? A string of murders had taken place in the town years ago when I was young. They'd found the murderer, and he spouted such nonsense about demons and dark lords that he'd been given prison for life instead of the death penalty. They'd ruled him clinically insane. He had said there were more murderers like him, but had refused to give names, even for a plea bargain. He'd been killed by a fellow inmate not long after he was imprisoned.

"Wendy, go talk to Mrs. Marshall, okay?" I said, my voice slightly stern. Truth was, as sweet as Wendy was, I was worried she was going to crack one day and hurt someone.

Wendy snatched my arm in a sudden movement that made me scream. She grabbed my arm tight until it hurt. My eyes went wide with fear and surprise.

"Miss Kayla! Don't go to the woods alone. Don't go anywhere alone!" she shouted. "It's not safe."

"Let go!" I screamed, wrenching my arm from her and stepping back.

She looked stricken and shrank back into herself, assuming again her usual sunken-in stance and quiet demeaner.

My voice trembled when I spoke next, relieved that she hadn't done anything worse in front of the class. "Mrs. Marshall's office. Now. Let's go."

I walked her up to the counselor's office in silence and as she walked in, she looked back at me once with a sad frown.

"Wendy—I'm sorry. You just scared me. It's going to be okay, though, all right? You and me: We're okay. Just keep your appointments with Mrs. Marshall."

Wendy shook her head slowly and whispered under her breath. "Be careful. Don't go out alone."

After my harrowing day at work, I spent the rest of the day shopping and wandering the historic downtown district of Edgar Falls so I wouldn't have to go home to another lecture from my parents. I bought a jagged-cut sparkling amethyst from the new age gift shop and pocketed it to give to Nora later as a peace offering. She used to collect them. It was a little bigger than my fist and I was barely able to fit it in my pocket. I smiled, because I knew Nora would make some kind of crude joke about my bulging pocket. It was nice to have her goofy, blunt personality in my life again.

Late at night, after Nora got off work at the hospital where she worked, she and I started on our walk. She had chosen the Edgar Falls Park, the namesake for the town, to be our hiking location. As I got out of my car and walked toward the entrance of the hiking trail, I watched the wind whip the Edgar Falls Park sign. It was a cheap sign: Canvas strung with bungee cord to two poles. The wind made it bounce in a crazy, erratic manner that disturbed me, almost as if it were trying to get my attention or trying to warn me of something.

"Is it me, or are you happy to see me?" Nora quipped, glancing at the ridiculous swollen pocket of my jogging pants where I'd stashed the amethyst.

I jumped at her voice, having been entranced by the jumping sign.

"So happy," I said, sticking my tongue out at her and twisting my face into a goofy grimace.

Her comment made me think about my pants, though, and the thought made me unhappy. I'd had to get new jogging pants just for this walk. I didn't fit in any of my size sixes anymore. The fact that I was wearing a size twelve had been embarrassing, but it was better than exercising in jeans.

The tall grass brushed our hips as we entered the forest path that we used to take almost daily, before I'd become depressed. The familiar feel of it all was comforting. I felt my mind become calm as I listened to the steady thuds of our feet hitting the ground, punctuated by the sharp crunches of plant matter. The hoot of an owl startled us both, and we giggled.

It was eerie weather, with a deep fog settling over the trees with humid air that was thick and hard to breath. Nora had a flashlight to see in the dark, but I tripped on several rocks anyway, earning me several rounds of good-natured heckling from Nora. As we continued to walk down the hiking trail and the trees became thicker and closer together, I forgot about the amethyst I wanted to give Nora, because my mind was preoccupied with just breathing.

I was embarrassed by how much I huffed and puffed. Was I really that out of shape that walking wore me out?

"You take up smoking recently or something?" Nora said, referring to my labored breezing and wheezing.

I started to laugh off the comment, but then I heard a shuffling sound far off to our left. I froze.

"Nora," I said sharply. "Point your flashlight over there. I heard something."

I pointed into the darkness where I heard the sound.

"Ugh. When did you get so jumpy?" she said, "It's probably just a squirrel or a possum or something. We're in the woods. Animals do live here, you know."

The sound repeated itself: four distinct shuffles through grass and leaves. Each one sounded louder and closer.

"There it is again," I said.

"It's nothing," Nora said, waving the flashlight around in exaggerated erratic arcs. She started walking, leaving me several yards behind her.

I stayed still, trying to listen.

"Come on, let's keep going. You're just making excuses, so you can catch your—" Nora froze with a surprised expression on her face as the light caught on a human face lurking in the darkness behind a nearby oak tree.

We both shrieked at seeing the man's face, which had a loose, odd-looking smile peering out from under a blue ball cap. The man's eyes were shrouded in the darkness and shadow of the hat's bill.

"Abe?" Nora said, her voice trembling. "W-what are you doing out here?"

The man didn't answer, and Nora gasped as her flashlight flickered and then went out.

Then she screamed.

I couldn't see, because my eyes hadn't adjusted to the absence of the flashlight, but I heard more rustling and an inhuman growl come from the man.

I heard a sickening slap and a thud. Nora was shrieking and the man was grunting with effort.

My heart raced and my mind reeled. Was this really happening to us?

"Run, Kayla!" Nora gasped, her voice sounding choked.

Without thinking, I sprinted toward the sound of her voice. My legs were as supple as springs as I ran to my friends aid. I flung myself to the ground where she'd dropped the flashlight and I swung it around to where the man was wrestling Nora to the ground. I saw the scene in flashes: The blood dripping from Nora's forehead, the ugly expression on the man's face, the red scrapes on the man's forearms where Nora had scratched and hit and bit him.

I swung the flashlight back and struck the man in the head, hoping I wouldn't miss my target in the dark, wild tangle of struggling arms and limbs.

The flashlight made contact and I heard a sickening crunch, yet the man didn't shout or cry out. He just turned with a slow, determined resolve and grasped the flashlight in his hand. His arm was strong, much stronger than it should have been for a man of his advanced age, and he yanked it away from me, throwing the flashlight far out of reach.

I backed away, feeling helpless and wondering if this would be my last night alive.

Nora was whimpering and cradling one of her arms. It was jutting out at an odd angle, as if it had been broken.

As if things couldn't get any more bizarre or terrifying, he started chanting in a low, menacing voice as he closed in on me with his hands outstretched. There was an eldritch gleam in his eyes, and the language he spoke was one I'd never heard before. The moonlight gave his sweaty skin a sickly yellow gleam.

Even though I couldn't understand the words, I knew that what I was facing was pure evil.

So I ran.

I ran, focusing on the sound of my own breathing until I settled into a familiar rhythm. My feet, my hips, and my lungs worked in a holy communion to propel me out of darkness. It all came back to me then, despite my terrible physical condition. I could hear the man keeping pace behind me, ready to pounce, but I pushed on.

Once a runner, always a runner.

Then my foot snagged a log and I tumbled onto my face.

"Obey," he commanded in a gravelly voice. "My master requires your life."

I flipped myself on my back and watched as he leaned in close. I waited until his hands were almost around my neck.

Then I pulled the amethyst out from my pocket and struck him in the mouth. Spittle and blood flew from the opposite side of his mouth almost immediately.

The scariest thing was that he didn't react at all. He seemed to feel no pain. His tongue worked around his mouth for a moment, and then he spat a bloody tooth onto the ground as if it were something as banal as a watermelon seed.

I reared my legs back and kicked hard on his chest with both legs, and the momentum sent him flailing away. While he was off balance I struck again with the amethyst, this time on his temple.

And again, and again.

The jagged stone drew blood wherever I struck, but he didn't scream. In the dark, I saw strings of something hanging off the amethyst. It took me several moments to realize they were pieces of skin that had been scraped from his face by the blows.

He laughed.

Even as he crumpled to the ground, he continued to laugh. From this new perspective I saw that I had left a huge dent in his head with the stone. I felt a high-pitched scream come out of my throat unbidden at the sight.

He shouldn't have been conscious with an injury like that.

As the blood seeped out of the wound, he ceased chuckling for a moment and his eyes started to droop closed.

"It won't stop," he whispered, "I'm only a vessel." Then his eyes closed. They stayed closed, and I resisted the urge to keep pounding away at his lifeless body, just to be sure he was dead.

I jumped at the sound of rustling behind my shoulder.

"It's just me," Nora said, her voice still shaky. "I'm going to go get the flashlight. Stay put."

After a few moments I heard Nora scream.

I ran toward the light of the flashlight and she looked at me with a horrified expression.

"What?" I said.

In reply, she merely pointed the flashlight at a spot on the ground. There was a dainty-looking hand peeking out from under leaves. That was when the decayed smell hit me.

I struggled to control my gag response, but I failed and had to whirl around quickly and vomit in a bush.

"I think we found the missing woman," Nora whispered. She put a hand on my shoulder.

"Guess we should call the police," I said mechanically.

Nora pulled out her phone and started to dial.

"Nora," I said, gripping her uninjured arm hard. I was seized by a strange and macabre kind of joy despite the circumstances, "Nora, I *ran*."

"I know," she said with a wan smile, still holding her injured arm in an awkward position. The reassuring sound of her ringing phone filled the night air.

"Nora," I said, holding the blood-slicked amethyst up in my trembling hand. "I got this for you."

She gave me an unreadable look and I dropped the gore-covered rock. She let out a strange, strangled laugh and shook her head. We hugged.

We held each other, trembling with sobs and hollow laughter, until the cops and the EMTs arrived.

***

Note: An altered version of this story was produced on The NoSleep Podcast.

8

Rosewater

Dear Frostbend Park Board and Frostbend Gardeners Association,

It is with great sadness that I inform you of a matter regarding my future participation in the gardening community. I almost left without this explanation, but I feel a responsibility to recount my reasons for leaving. Please know it has nothing to do with the integrity of your prestigious and helpful organizations, which are, in my opinion, the crowning jewels of the Frostbend community. With that said, I'll start at the beginning.

The title of Champion Gardener is an honor bestowed upon one lucky candidate every three years. In our little town, I always felt it was akin to winning the lottery. The person who receives this award gets all the city gardening contracts, and most of the gardening business from the citizens follows as well. After keeping the title for ten years, I was bested by an upstart. Me, Priscilla Henry, conquered by Caroline Verdi. Can you believe it? Well, of course you can. You probably voted for her roses.

Well, my hybrid tea roses have never let me down before, and I tried to assure myself that it wouldn't happen again this year. But I never planned what happened next. It happened *organically*, if you will. I invited Caroline over for tea at my country estate. The invitation was presented as an olive branch and a truce in our quiet rivalry.

"Come to my place. We'll talk shop and trade secrets," I'd said.

"I'd be delighted! I'll bring a bottle of wine," she'd answered.

Well, it wasn't a lie. We did talk about our strategies for cross-breeding and cultivating roses. I got dozens of tips about how she created those show-stopping hybrids. I got tips from her about how to mend holes from wood-boring insects, how to keep rot from taking the leaves. You'd be surprised to know how much I enjoyed my social hour with my mortal enemy. I enjoyed her company so much so that I almost left things there. I almost let her go. She gave me some ingenious tips for making use of leftover rose hips and how to make rose petal jam, after all. She smelled of rosewater perfume, and when I complimented her on it she described how it is made from the petals. Still, no matter how many tips she gave me, I couldn't stop the hatred coursing through my blood.

But given a second chance, with all I now know, I would have let her get into her car and leave.

Instead, under the guise of refilling our ice bucket, I came up from behind and thrashed her in the head with the metal watering can.

It may be hard to believe, but it wasn't planned. There was something about the way she twisted up her mouth when she gazed at a little brown corner of my creeping phlox. That look rattled something loose in my chest. At that moment, I grabbed the can and swung it in a wide arc. There wasn't even time for her to be surprised. That loose thing rattling around in my chest wouldn't allow me to stop at the watering can, and I grabbed a nearby shovel and started wailing away at her with that as well.

After my vision cleared and I became more settled, I stared down at her ruined body in shock. What was there to do now? It wasn't like I could just toss her on the burn pile like she was a tall weed I chopped down.

Chopped.

I let that word linger in my mind.

My eyes veered to the woodchipper in the nearby field. Perhaps I could hide her in plain sight. I dragged her by the legs through the tall grass. When I first tried to get her into the woodchipper, I found she was too much to put in all at once. Her limbs were unwieldy, her head unbalanced and lolling. I had to get the ax and cut her into smaller, more manageable pieces. It was filthy work, and that's something, coming from a gardener who has her fingers in the dirt all day.

When I turned the woodchipper on and threw the first piece in, I hadn't expected the thick spray of blood. I suppose I'd been expecting dry splinters, like wood. Once she'd lost consciousness, she'd seemed less and less like a person to me, and more like an object. So, it wasn't hard to do. It felt familiar to me, like dealing with a meddlesome tree that was growing where it wasn't supposed to. The wet sounds of the chipping procedure reminded me that this material was different, though. A combination of the sounds of squelching meat and the cracks of splintering bones greeted every hunk of Caroline that I threw into the hopper. The worst of it was the clogs. Sticking and struggling with its load, the machine groaned and halted to a stop every few moments. Caroline's head proved especially problematic and needed some extra helping along with a stout hammering.

After what seemed like an entire day, I finally had a pile of manageable material. I looked at the pile and held some of the ground meat in my hand. The red color reminded me of the bags of new red mulch I'd just purchased. Another stroke of brilliance. The pile that used to be Caroline was organic material, so I made it part of my new mulch blend. Mixed thoroughly with the red mulch, it was nearly impossible to tell that there was a secret ingredient.

But it seemed like my roses did detect the change. Soon after I applied the fresh mulch to my flower beds, I discovered a robust response from my roses. The blooms exploded and multiplied exponentially. Granted, a few folks came by the house and asked about the bad smell, but it was easy enough to blame that on the compost pile. For myself, I began making rosewater as Caroline had taught me. I dabbed it under my nose to keep the stench of rot at bay.

In only a week, I had a rainbow of every color rose, with the bushes full and bursting with petals and the stems bending with the weight of their bounty. It attracted so many pollinating insects that I could hear their happy buzzing from inside my house. It was a remarkable sight: those fragrant, pastel roses held aloft the sherbet-orange sunset like a banner. It was almost worth what happened next.

I thought that was the end of it until a week later when a mound of that red mulch appeared under my window out of nowhere. I went out and around the house and looked up at the mountainous mound. My first thought was that someone knew what I'd done. They had taken the evidence and planted it right where I'd be sure to see it. But that was ridiculous. Nobody had seen, and even if they had, why wouldn't they just go to the police?

With no answers, I did the only thing I could do and I took a shovel and wheelbarrow to it, determined to return the potent mulch to my roses. However, I was met with a surprise when I arrived.

Every rose had died overnight without the mulch's mysterious magic. I gawked at stalks turned gray and brittle and touched the dry and crumbling flowers. All color was gone and with it all the garden's vibrance. Black edges curled the edges of petals like burn marks and putrid yellow spots of disease speckled the few leaves that hadn't already fallen to the ground. I fell to my knees and mourned them. Some of the plants had been a decade old. In the end, I carried every ounce of mulch back to the devasted garden in the dull hope that it could revive them. It was at this point that I began to suspect there was something left of Caroline. Who else would want me to see the potential of my plants in their greatest expression, only to make it that much more painful when it was razed to the ground?

The morning after, I awoke to a dark, damp pile over my face. I gasped to alertness and opened my eyes only to be met by an absence of light. The smell of rot filled my nostrils. I breathed by reflex and choked on bits and pieces of some mystery substance. Damp, coppery chunks lodged themselves in my throat, blocking all air. Flailing my arms, I clawed out of it, inch by inch. Once I'd freed my torso from the mound, I clambered free with wild desperation, emerging from the side of a great heap. I dug my index finger into my clogged throat and dragged free a chunk of raw meat. I wheezed and coughed and spat.

Next, I crawled to the door of my bedroom. There was a soft whimper from my mouth as I turned around. On the bed from which I'd narrowly escaped, was a hill of bloody red mulch. It tumbled down as I watched, staining the carpets and creeping forward like a rising tide. I stumbled out of the room, slammed the door, and locked the cursed pile inside.

I washed the blood off in the shower and went about my day like normal, avoiding the locked room. I tried not to sleep, but that night I succumbed to exhaustion and fell into a deep sleep on the couch.

That brings us to this morning. I did not wake to a dark heft of mulch on my body. There was no pile rising to meet my groggy eyes. Instead, I felt a wave of nausea. It was like a pile of stones were dropped into my gut, tumbling around and pushing my organs about inside me. The painful stomach tremors increased, stronger each second, until I leaned over the side of the couch and hurled. The relief I felt at releasing my stomach's contents was sublime, and yet it only lasted a moment before the next purge began. In between heaves and screams, I watched a profusion of red wood chips and mush building in a pile below my mouth. I must have thrown up for hours, too tortured to move or stand. And after the torturous passing of many hours, that mountain of mulch again faced me, this time fouled and soaked with bile. My throat was so sore that I could barely make a sound by the end.

"Caroline," I said in a hoarse whisper. My pink pajamas were splattered red. I wiped my dripping, drooling mouth and looked at my shaking crimson fingers. I'd underestimated Caroline once, and she'd beat me in the contest. And now? It appeared I'd underestimated her a second time.

What exactly was this woman capable of? What power of will did she have that she could still best me, even after her death? I had to admit, it was almost impressive.

I had to admit defeat then. I bought a gun.

The gun is waiting for me in the garden shed, and I'm going to use it to escape from this nightmare. I've got to end whatever game Caroline's playing with me before I find out what she has in store next. I'll be gone by the time you read this.

Perhaps Caroline and I are destined to feed the roses together. I have to say—I'm slightly impressed with her. Whoever finds this letter: can you turn me into mulch too? That might satisfy Caroline at last. Else I fear for this inertia of hers. What if the whole of Frostbend became swallowed in mulch? I can see it happening. You'd better do your best to appease her. She's grown more powerful in death than she ever was in life.

No doubt you'll be looking for Caroline's body. I'd tell you where to find the mulch, but it keeps moving. Last I saw, it was on the floor of my kitchen, but by tomorrow it might be somewhere else. Good luck with that. I have a feeling she'll find you anyway, so don't worry too much.

The bottom line is this: Please accept my resignation from the park board and the gardener's association, effective immediately. I understand that my demise implies my resignation, but I feel I owe an explanation for what you'll find here today. I can now leave knowing that I've left a warning about what is to come. I apologize for having gotten rid of my most obvious replacement on the board. Best of luck with your future gardens, and with the future of Frostbend. You're going to need it.

Sincerely,
Priscilla Henry
Champion Gardener from 2008-2018

P.S. Please excuse the horrible stains on this letter. If you've read my account, you understand that this has been a messy process, and I've run out of time to rewrite this. Caroline is coming, and I must be gone before she finds me. There's a crate in the garage containing bottles of rosewater. Help yourself. It smells amazing. When Caroline arrives, you might need it. She smells worse every day.

***

Florence looked up from the letter. His hands were shaking.

"You asked," Samantha said with a shrug. "I thought you should find out from me before it went through the gossip mill."

"Do you believe it?" he replied.

Samantha stretched her arms in the air before examining one of the roses on the bush in front of city hall. "Parts of it. I think she did kill her friend." She scoffed. "I don't think that the mulch was following her around everywhere if that's what you mean."

Florence nodded. "I was excited to take over for the Park Board, but this makes me feel a bit nervous. Are people really that cutthroat about it here?"

Samantha avoided his eyes. Her hands coaxed a crumbling leaf from a branch. "Relax. This is a small town. And things can be intense, sure, but Priscilla Henry was an outlier. She was going to hurt someone one way or another. It didn't have anything to do with the Park Board." She cupped a bit of mulch and tossed it in Florence's direction, showering him in wood chips.

"Hey!"

"See?" She grinned. "It's not going to get you." She glanced at her watch. "I've got to go pick my kid up from school. Can you finish up here?"

Florence nodded. "Yeah, I got it."

"Thanks." Samantha got into her car and drove off.

When Florence finished, it was near sunset. He was covered in sweat and wiped his forehead as he returned to the truck. As he passed the truck bed, something caught his eye. They had already emptied all the new mulch for the city hall project. Yet, there was mulch in the back of the truck. It was bright red and especially moist looking. And there was a smell that was fouler than anything Florence had ever smelled. He imagined it was what it would smell like if you opened a grave a few weeks after a burial.

He staggered back, and from the crack where the truck bed hinged open, he saw something that made him scream: A slow drip of dark red blood.

***

Note: This story was first published on Kindle Vella.

9

Welcome to Honeyhill Estates

All Erin Morgansen ever wanted was to belong somewhere, but as of this year, she was jobless and recently divorced. She had as many problems as she had freckles—and she had a lot of the latter. While married, she had applied to a sweepstakes for a free home in an exclusive housing society called Honeyhill Estates—the first of its kind in the United States. When she actually won the contest, it seemed like it all came at just the right time. And as she entered the wrought-iron gates of Honeyhill Estates on move-in day with her precious only daughter Skye, she thought she had finally found that sense of community she longed for, too.

One of the unique draws of Honeyhill Estates was that this elite housing society was built on an island. A single bridge connected it to the mainland, and it boasted a reputation as the most secure community in America because you had to have a pass to use the bridge. Becoming a resident of Honeyhill gave you exclusive access to the community movie theater, gym, shopping strip, multiple grocery stores, and other amenities right on the island. On this first day, someone was already waiting by the gate for their arrival and waved with a big smile as they let Erin's car through.

As they drove toward their new home, Erin and Skye admired the sharp-edged lawns with bright carpets of Bermuda grass set out like welcome mats. Most marvelous were the petunias and begonias dotting the window boxes like colorful candies. The houses were bricked in front with clean white siding, and every single one was the same. Skye squealed as they passed the movie theater and begged to go as soon as possible.

Adding to the picturesque view was the multitude of large green hills surrounding the homes and adding depth to the landscape. And all around Honeyhill, there was a lack of debris and an abundance of order. Quietness reigned, even at midday.

When the car made a turn, flashing a side view of dozens of the identical houses at once, Erin was reminded of a row of carefully stacked dominos. Skye commented that they looked like white teeth.

Once in the driveway of their new home, a tan woman in capris and a frothy pink top bustled over. Her eyes were a startling electric blue color, and her arms cradled a wicker basket tied with a jaunty crimson bow.

"Welcome, Morgensens! I'm Stephanie Williams, but you can call me Steph! I'm the president of the homeowner's association. So, if you have any questions, I'm happy to help!"

"Nice to meet you," Erin said, putting out her hand for a shake. Instead of taking her hand, Steph pulled Erin into a solid hug, enveloping her in the overwhelming smell of Steph's freesia perfume.

"Don't be afraid to get close," Steph said into Erin's hair.

Erin gritted her teeth, using all her self-control not to pull away. The cloying smell of the perfume left her dizzy even after the hug was over.

"I just came by to give you this Honeyhill welcome basket."

"That's so kind of you," Erin said. But when she looked down into the wicker basket, there wasn't the expected heap of fruit or baked goods.

"I know it's not your standard apple pie. But it's much more useful." She pulled out the items, handling them over like treasured artifacts. "This is the standard set of security cameras."

Erin regarded the cameras with their cords and baggies filled with mounting hardware.

"I thought this was a safe place."

"Yes, and how do you think we came to be this safe?"

"Well, this is sweet, but I don't think we'll need it. Cameras like this sort of creep me out."

Steph kept smiling, but the intensity flared, much like when a power surge causes the lights to get brighter. "Trust me. You'll love the peace of mind. Just have your husband hang them up when he gets here. Two outside and two inside. There's a little red mark showing where they should go."

"There won't be any husband joining us."

Steph didn't miss a beat, nor did she apologize. "Anyways, you need to put them up. If you don't, I don't think your neighbors will be too happy. It creates a dead zone, a place where people can hide. You wouldn't want to be responsible for bringing crime here, would you?"

"No, of course not but—"

"Nobody's ever refused it before," Steph said. A wrinkle appeared between her eyebrows.

It was the first day. Did Erin really want to single herself out as an outsider already?

"Of course," she sighed.

The wrinkle on Steph's face smoothed out and she grabbed the next item, a small piece of tech that fit in the palm of her hand.

"This is a GPS tracker. I'll just pop it on the wheel well." She leaned over and affixed the device to Erin's car. "Now, you'll always be protected by our community. If you break down or have a wreck, we can instantly come and help and provide you with a rental. Or if by some chance somebody stole your car and took it off the island, we'd have no trouble getting it back."

Erin felt uneasy about having her movements tracked. Still, she didn't have anything to hide, and she'd already agreed to the security cameras. Maybe it wouldn't be so bad to have people looking out for her now that she was a single mom.

Steph stood up and smoothed the front of her capris. "Plus, once your daughter here starts driving, I'm sure you'll appreciate knowing she's where she's supposed to be."

Erin nodded and smiled.

"I'm sure you'll be reading the full list of HOA regulations, but just so you know, the most important one is the maintenance of our lawns." She took her finger and pointed to the 3-inch mark. "The grass must be three inches. No more. No less." She laughed. "Sometimes it takes time to get the mower blades in the right position, so we sometimes let it slide if it's a little less." She winked at Skye.

Erin burst out laughing, all her previous tension fading. "Oh my goodness. You're completely messing with me. I'm so relieved." She laughed so hard that she snorted a little, and she was too relieved to even be that embarrassed about it, even though she sensed Skye wearing a mortified glower.

Steph didn't say anything. The ruler stayed in her hands, her finger pointing to the number three. Her smile dropped.

"We're quite serious about lawn care here."

Erin realized that Steph was speaking in earnest, and she tried to recover. "Of course you are. I'm sorry."

Steph's unflappable smile returned as she reached into her pocket for a business card. "Most of us use this lawn care service." She smiled, then waved another card before Erin's face. "And this is your key card for the access gate at the bridge. This is your way on and off the island."

"Thanks for that." Erin took the cards and stuffed them into her jeans pocket.

They exchanged further excruciating pleasantries, including the question of what Erin did for a living—nothing at the moment, given that she'd been a stay-at-home mom before the divorce. The only thing keeping them afloat was the child support payments for Skye, but Erin planned to begin job hunting the moment they settled in. Judging by the multitude of luxury businesses on Honeyhill, Erin thought it wouldn't take long to find a job right there on the island.

Steph just did a little *ahh* expression with extremely high eyebrows. Erin began to feel like she and her daughter didn't represent the *standard* family of Honeyhill Estates.

"Oh!" Steph said, looking at her pink smartwatch. "It's almost 2 o'clock. That's when the mail ferry comes each day. I've got to get some things sent off today, so I'd better get going."

"Mail ferry?"

"Yes! It's the fastest way to get things to and from the island. And," Steph continued, smiling down at her cell phone. "I just texted a guy from the homeowner's association and he is more than happy to set up your cameras today."

When she then turned and popped open Erin's mailbox. Erin desperately hoped that she wasn't about to explain the mailbox too.

"Well look at that!" Steph exclaimed. "You've got a little somethin' in there already." She pulled out a small white envelope with the Honeyhill logo: an oversized *H* with curly vines creeping up the sides, all of it sitting on top of a stylized, hill-like curve. The logo was the color of goldenrods, bright and cheery.

Erin took the letter and opened it.

Dear Mr. and Mrs. Morgensen

We regret to inform you that your lawn has surpassed the 3-inch limit. Please see the attached invoice for $100. Please pay your fee within two weeks of receipt of this notice to reinstate your good standing with the neighborhood.

Sincerely,

Honeyhill Estates Homeowner's Association

"How can my grass be out of compliance? We just got here!"

"Well, you *were* responsible for the lawn from the date of your title transfer, which I think was about two weeks ago maybe?" She said this innocently as if she wasn't sure if she was correct.

With a tone that was only slightly apologetic, Steph repeated, "We're quite serious about lawncare here," as if that explained everything. She handed over a manual that was the size of a small novel. "Rules and regulations for the Honeyhill Estates community. Everything you need to know is right here."

Erin took the book in hand and turned it over, taking in its depth.

"Awesome!" she said, which was the opposite of what she had been thinking.

"Take care!" Steph called as Erin closed the door behind herself and Skye. It was said in a friendly tone, but some part of Erin's brain heard another message, a hidden threat behind Steph's upbeat front.

Once inside, Erin found herself leaning against the back of the door as if she were afraid that Steph might try to bust inside. When she noticed she was doing this, she shook her head and forced herself to walk over to the window, just to prove to herself that she wasn't afraid.

Screwing her mouth up into a frown, she flipped the regulation manual to the table of contents to find the part about the damn grass. As she did, the paper's edge sliced into her finger. Yelping, she dropped the book on the ground. When she picked it back up, there was a drop of blood on the page.

And then, despite multiple protestations from Skye about her dire need to stave off imminent starvation, Erin stood in front of the bay window for a long time, watching the distant view of ocean waves coming in and out past the dozens of black gable roofs. Her eyes traced the curves of the great green mounds of earth that were Honeyhill's namesake. All the while, she set to work convincing herself of the merits of Honeyhill, mentally repeating them like a mantra: how beautiful this view was, how much better than their old apartment with the crowded quarters and footsteps above them.

As Erin's empty stomach growled, she thought of the woman who had lived next to her apartment, Mrs. Bertolini, who never hesitated to knock on their door and ask if everything was okay when Erin and her ex-husband had been arguing. It drove Erin up the wall with annoyance. Mrs. Bertolini had always filled her patio with potted plants and Skye watered them twice on Tuesdays in the hot summer months when the woman went out of town to get her dialysis treatments. In return, Erin found a homemade casserole on her patio on Wednesday nights. Today was Wednesday, the first summer Wednesday where there would be no casserole.

Heavy in her hands was the book of rules, and her blood had dried on it by the time she put it down.

***

Time passed. Weeks. Then a month. The letter about the grass was only the first of many. Erin's fingers began to tremble as she neared the mailbox in these days. She started a habit of letting the mail pile up until the mouth of the box couldn't close. It was like her mailbox had contracted a sickness, spewing and puking paper.

All this was because almost daily there was a message from the HOA. One day, it was about the color of her curtains, which were barely visible behind her blinds, not complying. On another, it was about dirt on the house's siding. Later, a complaint about a single, forgotten weed growing under one of her palm trees. A garbage can left outside of the garage for too long. She had read the book cover-to-cover so many times, but the homeowner's association seemed determined to catch her somehow. And despite the HOA president knowing full well that Erin was single, the letters were always addressed to *Mr. and Mrs.* Morgansen.

For every letter balanced in the teetering pile on Erin's kitchen table, there was an accompanying fine. Now, as she balanced her budget, the expenses were catching up with the child support coming in. Erin had begun her job search on the island, but as the letters piled up, she began to feel she needed temporary escapes from Honeyhill.

She began to search for jobs on the mainland exclusively, just to go someplace with fewer rules and where it felt easier to breathe. Each day after Skye set off to the community school, Erin took the bridge off the island to job hunt on the mainland, but so far had no success.

But if Erin was languishing in the neighborhood, at least Skye seemed to be excelling at the small middle school, and especially on the track team. Erin didn't understand a lot of the lingo, but she heard a lot of chatter from Sky about new *personal bests* and the best numbers on the *splits*. Overall, the impression was that Skye was the fastest runner on the team. And at least this was a consolation to Erin for all her sacrifices. It was the only one she had.

So when, about two months into their stay at Honeyhill, Skye had her first track meet, Erin was enthusiastic about going to show her support. She prepared a slightly over-the-top outfit, with every single item coordinated in the green and gold of the Honeyhill Middle School colors. At this event, with the cheering families and the energy of youth in the air, things felt more like how Erin had expected life at Honeyhill to feel: exuberant and full. During the meet, at which Skye had won several ribbons in multiple categories, Erin was thrilled to be pulled into a conversation with the other adults.

Erin even made some new friends. The woman, Capella was short and had olive skin and dark brown hair. Capella's husband, Ethan, was pale and tall with no hair on his face or head. Although the couple didn't have any children of their own, they lived right next door to the track and liked to watch the meets. They invited Erin and Skye over for dinner the next day, and Erin heartily accepted.

Everything would have been perfect the day of the track meet if it hadn't been for one thing that occurred right at the end. When one of the runners stood by Erin, slugging water and breathing heavily over his knees, she noticed that his eyes were trained on the tall hills in the distance that were so plentiful at Honeyhill.

"Are you okay?" Erin said. "Your face is as red as a tomato!"

The boy answered without looking at her. "My grandpa is in that middle one," he said, pointing to a trio of giant hills.

Erin swallowed hard. "Excuse me?"

"You don't belong here. You should leave." He looked at Erin in the eyes then, holding her gaze. He twisted his hands in an agitated manner.

Suddenly, the boy's mother emerged from the crowd and yanked the child away before he could say more. She didn't even look at Erin but whispered her rebukes feverishly into the boy's ear as they stormed off to the parking lot.

As Erin and Skye made their way back to their car, they were elbowed and shoved in the crowd as everyone vied for the first chance at getting back home. She tried not to think of how uneasy the boy had made her feel.

Erin rubbed her arm and thought of Harold, who worked the register at the corner grocery store by her old apartment. Harold had started carrying Erin's groceries to her car when she'd become pregnant with Skye. He had never actually stopped doing it, even though Erin no longer needed his help. It annoyed Erin when she was in a hurry because he liked to take his time and chat.

That night, she missed Harold. She would have liked the distraction of a long chat.

***

The house of Capella and Ethan Thompson looked like every other house on the island, and that was just the problem. It was impossible to find. Rows and rows of identical two-story houses with white siding, black roofs, and matching brick mailboxes, flanked by green slabs of rectangular hedges. After fifteen minutes of wandering through the labyrinthine streets, Erin turned on her phone's GPS, giving up on her own sense of direction. She muttered and cursed at the machine under her breath when it wouldn't cooperate, finally throwing the phone roughly into the passenger seat.

She turned her eyes to her daughter's face in the rear-view mirror.

"Did you find a book for your report yet?"

"No. All the books at the library were boring."

"Well, it's due in a few days, so you need to pick something. Just pick anything."

Erin thought of Kyle, who worked at the public library where they'd moved from. He checked out patrons extremely slowly because he was high most of the time. On the other hand, he always took the time to give Skye and Erin personalized book recommendations that were right in line with their interests. If Kyle was here, Skye's report would already be finished.

Erin sighed and refocused on finding the Thompson house. With no distinguishable landmarks, she had a dizzying sense of being lost in a maze that had been designed to confuse on purpose. Whenever Erin expected to find a cul-de-sac to turn around in, she met with a turn into another street instead. When she felt she was getting close to a turn, the road rounded out into a dead end. There was a queasy feeling building in her stomach. Finally, with her heart thudding in her ears, she pulled over to the roadside, parked, and grabbed her phone again.

"Mom, you okay?" Skye asked. "Are we lost?"

"Oh, honey," Erin answered with a laugh that sounded uneasy, "of course not. I'm just having a little trouble finding the house. They all look the same here, don't they?"

"Yeah." Skye leaned forward so she could meet her mother's eyes over the center console. "I talked to dad on the phone last night and he said Honeyhill sounds like a place where originality goes to die."

"Look," Erin said, talking through the lump in her throat. "I know that people are different here and it's nothing like our old apartment. But can you just give it a fair chance?"

"Like you were fair to dad?"

Erin's face went hot and she gripped the steering wheel harder to keep her face from betraying how angry she was. Erin had cheated; it was true. What she hadn't realized was that cheating on her husband would mean her spouse would forever be absolved of any responsibility for what he'd contributed to the dissolution of their relation-ship. Erin had provided an easy label to put on the whole situation, *infidelity*, and people never inquired further about the situation. They didn't need to or want to.

"Is your math homework done?" Erin said in an overly bright tone. "Or do I need to ask Capella if she has a quiet space where you can concentrate?"

"You're just changing the subject!" Skye spat.

In lieu of a reply, Erin grabbed the gear stick and jerked the car into reverse. There was no warning at all before the tires met with a hard solid thunk. There was a moment of shock when Erin's stomach leaped into her throat. Then she whipped the car forward, parked, and burst out of the door.

The ruined body of an orange tabby cat met her eyes as she emerged from the car. Its bloodied and flattened body twitched once before going completely still. She felt the urge to do something, or call someone, but at the same time, Erin could see that all hope of life had fled this little creature's body.

Before Erin could tell her not to, Skye clambered out of the car and gawked at the bloodied animal.

"You killed it!" She wailed.

"It was an accident," Erin answered in a quiet voice. She put a hand on her stomach and bent near the cat to see if she could find a name-plate on its collar. Just as she was reaching out to grab it, a voice star-tled her from behind.

"Oh, that's it for him, isn't it?" Capella said from the sidewalk. Her voice seemed lighter than it should have been, as if she were talking about a ruined piece of plastic patio furniture rather than someone's beloved pet. "Glad you found the house."

Erin almost fell over from her crouched position on the asphalt as she whipped her head around. Somehow, she'd managed to stumble upon the right house. "I'm so sorry," she began to say, stumbling over her words. "It was an accident."

"Please, come in. I'll have Ethan take care of it before we have dinner."

"Whose cat was it?" Erin said, unable to tear her eyes away from the mangled animal.

"Mine," Capella said. There was no visible emotion.

Erin groaned. "This is awful. We'll just go home and we can discuss how we can repay you after you've had time to grieve."

"No," Cappella said, her eyes wide, almost fearful. "Please. We need the company tonight." She approached and put a hand on Erin's shoulder. The hand was trembling.

Capella's insistence repulsed Erin, but another part of her felt compelled to stay. As a longtime resident, she hoped Capella could tell her how to get off the HOA's nastygram list. And she was still uneasy about what boy said about the hills. Maybe Capella could clear things up and say it was just a creepy story kids told to scare each other.

By the time Erin and Skye made their way into Capella's kitchen, Ethan had already plated up the food—spaghetti and meatballs. The hunks of meat swimming in red sauce would normally have been appetizing, but Erin fought her gag reflex, thinking of the pieces of the cat that had been sheared off by the tires. As she leaned on the kitchen island for support, she couldn't help but notice that someone had already emptied two full bottles of cabernet sauvignon, carelessly discarding the corks on the floor. Another full bottle was chilled and waiting with small beads of condensation running down its neck. Small splatters of dark red welled from the snaking veins of the Carrara marble countertop. Someone had poured these drinks in a hurry.

The steadily rising tide of unease threatened to take Erin over completely. But she was in so deep now, so entrenched in this dinner, that she couldn't think of a way out. If running over a cat hadn't gotten her out of this, nothing would.

After a dinner that proceeded largely in awkward silence, Erin sent Skye to the living room to finish her math homework. Once Skye left the room, Capella closed off the room by shutting the top of the

Dutch door between the two areas. She turned to Erin and reduced her voice to a furtive whisper.

"That cat was as good as dead before you even moved here."

Erin was stunned. Before she could say a word, Capella put up a finger to silence her, and took a long swill of wine, swishing it audibly around her mouth. When she spoke again, there was a rancid purple sheen on her teeth.

"The HOA doesn't allow cats," she said, looking at Ethan. "But we thought we could keep him a secret as long as he stayed indoors." She laughed. "What were we thinking, Ethan?"

Ethan didn't say anything. He stood, pushed in his chair, and left the room, closing the door behind him. The sound of his footsteps carried up the stairs, presumably to their bedroom. Erin watched Capella drink more wine.

"They found out somehow," she continued. "I think it's the cameras. For our security? Bullshit. Somebody from the association is watching the feed at all times. How else would they know? We never took him outside. We stopped having people over at our house. He was indoor only. Nobody could have known otherwise."

Erin had forced herself to eat a few bites of the food and she now regretted it. A tremor started deep in her belly and her meal tumbled around uncomfortably upon hearing this story. A fantom scent of freesia blew past her memory as she recalled what Steph had said about the cameras: *Nobody has ever refused them before.*

"Surely they can't do that," Erin said.

"And now," Capella said, swirling the glass in her hand, "people are whispering about how we're *going on holiday.* Us. I never thought it would happen to us. So you'll forgive us if we're not ourselves tonight."

"Well," Erin said, confused and hopeful to change the subject. "A vacation will do you good. Maybe some of the drama will be better by the time you get back."

Capella gave her a look of startled disbelief. For the first time since they'd entered the dining room, she put her wine glass down. "You're so new, aren't you?" Tears leaked from her eyes. "There's so much you don't know. We've lived here for seven years, so we've seen and heard more than we should have. You shouldn't be talking to me, as new as you are. I'm going to get you in trouble."

"What do you mean? What kind of things have you seen?"

"I shouldn't have asked you here. Thank you for the company," Capella slurred, pulling a new bottle of wine from the fridge. It was a wonder that she was even able to stand at this stage, and she was far too drunk to give Erin any useful information. "And don't worry about that cat. Worry about yourself and that beautiful little girl of yours."

"No problem," Erin said honestly. Worrying was something she excelled at, and with each moment she spent at Honeyhill, she found herself doing it more.

When she finally arrived home that night with Skye asleep in the backseat, she decided to remove the GPS tracker from her car. After exiting the vehicle, there was a moment where she thought she smelled freesia again. But then the smell soured and transformed into something foul and rotting. She saw a piece of bloodied orange hair still clinging to her car's front tire and her stomach finally gave. She had no choice but to spew her dinner in the front yard, spaghetti sauce dripping all over the perfect Bermuda grass.

***

Once she'd recovered from feeling ill and had removed the tracker, two things became strikingly clear for Erin: she had made the worst mistake of her life, and she'd brought Skye right into the middle of it. Screw selling the house first. Something was wrong here, and they had to get out. That night she coached Skye through packing her most treasured belongings. They would take only what would fit in their four-door sedan and not worry about the rest.

Early in the morning, she and Sky drove to the gate. She waved her pass in front of the sensor. Every other day this week, when Erin had left to go on job interviews on the mainland, there had been a dulcet tone and a friendly green light preceding the gate opening. This time there was a sharp buzz and a red light instead. The gate remained closed.

Skye began to ask what was wrong, but Erin didn't answer. She just waved the card repeatedly, as if expecting a different result. The only response was a series of sharp buzzes.

"Come on!" she said, beating the sensor with her fist. "You've got to be kidding me!"

Finally, she let her forehead drop to the steering wheel. Tears of frustration sprang in her eyes, but before she could let them fall, she saw a quiet black car drive up behind them in her rearview mirror. In the driver's seat, a pair of cobalt-blue eyes were pinning Erin with their gaze.

Erin didn't look up as she heard the click of Steph's kitten heels on the asphalt. As a drizzle of rain fell on the hot ground, the smell of freesia weaved itself through the petrichor and made Erin's stomach seize.

"You can't keep us prisoner here!" Erin called out. "Stop screwing around and open the gate."

Steph made a soft shushing sound, putting her hand on Erin's shoulder. The reflection of her slick white raincoat with its pink lining filled the surface of the side view mirror. "I thought you understood what we were trying to do here," she replied, and when Erin finally looked up, there was something resembling true regret in Steph's electric blue eyes. "To belong to any community, there is a contract. You give up the parts of yourself that don't serve the community, because you know that it's worth it." Her smile was unnerving.

"But of course we won't keep anyone in the community against their will," she said through her straight white teeth.

"This is not a community. This is a cult."

"Every community is a cult in its own way," Steph said, digging her fingernails into Erin's shoulder. "The only difference is that here, the rules are made plain. Everywhere else you're left to figure it out on your own. Things happen and happen to you, and you never know the reason why. Here, the rules keep you safe. Out there, there are no guarantees."

"We're leaving," Erin said. The bluster of a building thunderstorm whipped through the open car window, slicking her hair over her eyes and mouth.

Steph nodded agreeably. "I only ask that you come to the community center for an exit interview. It will help us make things better for future residents to get your feedback."

"No. We're leaving right now. Open the gate."

"We'll worry about that after the interview." Her eyes narrowed and she gestured over her shoulder. Two muscular men, one of whom Erin remembered from her camera installation, emerged from the back of Steph's car.

***

Steph had somehow managed to assemble the entire HOA board and a smattering of other community members for the exit interview at the community center. There had to have been at least thirty people stuffed into the room as the heavy rainstorm throttled the windows. The lights inside the community center were glaringly bright, making the faces gathered around Skye and Erin seem garish.

Steph stood behind a podium, addressing the assembly. She wrapped one arm around Erin's shoulders and squeezed her with each word. "Let's give Erin and her daughter a warm farewell to show that there are no hard feelings."

As the woman said this, the attendees of the meeting stood and converged upon Erin and her daughter. The herd came close, encircling them, and then they embraced Erin and Skye. Their hugs were a little too firm. Erin didn't like to be touched much anyway, but these hugs felt suffocating. With each one, she noticed herself being pressed further toward the alcove behind the podium where a set of double doors waited

The hugs became more forceful, aggressive even.

"Back off!" Erin yelled.

Instead of backing off, the hugs transformed into overt violence, with shoves and pulls hard enough to bruise. The throng was leading her in one direction: toward that set of double doors in the back. The arms around Erin tightened and restrained her. She choked and gasped. The doors opened. Through the flurry of hands and arms, the first strange thing Erin noticed was the soundproofing material on the opposite side of the doors.

The second strange thing was the prison cells.

Between the cells, the corridor held wall sconces fashioned from mason jars, and a long rug snaked down the concrete floor. The metal bars on the cells were painted white like picket fences, and above each jail cell was a chalkboard sign with the prisoner's name chalked in an elegant swirling script. Her eyes caught on two cells marked *Capella Thompson* and *Ethan Thompson* but couldn't see inside them from her vantage point. Swinging from the ceiling beams above it all, a hand-painted sign bore the word *Holiday*. The sign sported a burlap bow.

Erin thrashed and scratched at the hands and arms dragging her down the stairs. She bit down on one of the arms. The copper taste of blood filled her mouth as a rubbery hunk of flesh came off in her teeth. Then, her chaotic flailing was ended by a hot flash of pain in her arm. Someone twisted it behind her back and slammed her into the floor.

From the ground, with the rug rough on her bruised cheek, Erin's eyes darted to Skye, who had become almost lost behind the throng, following at a distance.

Above the entry to the prison was a bronze clock decorated with fleur-de-lis. 2 o'clock—Erin noted—the time the mail ferry arrived. It was time for her little track star to put those legs to good use.

Erin breathed in and prepared to release the loudest scream of her life. As she roared, she thought her voice was rocking the foundation of the community center itself. Later she would realize it was a clap of thunder that had coincided with her cry.

"Skye! Run to the mail ferry!" Erin bellowed. Bloody spittle flew from her mouth as her eyes took in the streaking silhouette of her bright and beautiful daughter one last time. She held the image down with a pin in her mind: Skye's medium-taupe skin that echoed her father's deep brown. Her green eyes that were so much like Erin's. Her long arms and legs that were from neither parent but entirely Skye's own. She was perfect.

Erin tried not to remember the wide-eyed look of abject terror in Skye's face before she turned and ran, and the hands reaching out to grab her, but that became imprinted in memory too.

***

While *on holiday*, Erin liked to imagine Skye's life after escaping. She would never know if Skye got away but chose to believe it. She imagined Skye back in their old neighborhood where Harold at the corner grocery would talk too much and make Skye late for track practice. At the library, Kevin would suggest the perfect books, and Mrs. Bertolini would bring a casserole to the door on Wednesdays. Erin even imagined that Skye's father had a nice new girlfriend, and that Mrs. Bertolini didn't need to knock often to check on them because they were all happy.

Erin actively blocked the other possibility from her mind, the one where Skye didn't make it to the boat.

The other thing about being *on holiday* was that it gave her plenty of time to think about her mistakes. When she'd won the Honeyhill house sweepstakes, she'd rushed toward it without looking back. After the divorce, she was eager to cut ties with her old life. But in the process, she'd severed herself from a group of people tied by geography, common needs, and mutual hopes. A group of people who annoyed each other to death with their habits but still looked out for each other: A *community*. She'd had it all along and now would never get it back.

If her time *on holiday* proved successful, Erin could be reintegrated into Honeyhill one day. But if she messed up next time, she'd been warned that there would be no *holiday*. Next time, the only future she had to look forward to was the one where her body fed the well-manicured grasses of Honeyhill's mounds.

Death was the only way to escape Honeyhill. She was sure that if they ever did bury her in the mounds, she'd rake her pale bloodless arms through the disturbed, glutted earth and rise again, fueled by fury alone. Surely on such a night, a crisp, full moon would shine as she clawed out from that putrid hill, emerging stalwart, wretched, and cold. Flesh peeling, bones trembling, all sustaining her for just long enough to reach the ocean. There, waiting under the foam, her bones would spell a warning.

Each night when the bright lights in her cell kept her from sleeping, Erin imagined herself submerged in those ocean fathoms. There, the amber glow of Honeyhill's antique-imitation streetlamps could never reach her. There, nightmares and letters dissolved in the salty-sweet waters of eternal sleep.

***

Note: An altered version of this story was originally produced on the Nighty Night with Rabia Chaudry podcast.

10

The Skinless

Helena awoke mysteriously devoid of her skin. Everything on her body was red and pink. The sheets were damp and wet with fluids, and she felt more vulnerable than she ever had, with nothing but muscle holding her organs inside. She moved herself up to a seated position with care, feeling every movement with its individual, excruciating, and distinctive ache. Her eyes bulged as she watched the blood pulse in her tissues, watching with almost equal amounts of horror and fascination.

For these first few moments she assured herself it was only a dream. What other explanation could there be? She waited, as still as she could stay, to wake up. Eventually, the panic and fear ultimately won out, though. How could she not be afraid, when her own muscles and sinews were displayed before her, glistening and raw? Curiously, there was no blood, but there was pain. Any time even a small draft of wind went by, she doubled over with the pain from her exposed nerve endings.

Now she was going to the doctor because 911 had refused her request to be picked up and taken to the emergency room. She had to be kidding, they'd said. You didn't just wake up one day with your skin missing. She tried to explain that even so, she had woken up with her skin missing, but they'd told her to see a psychologist and then they had actually hung up on her.

Her boyfriend hadn't been much help either. She'd called him next, trying not to cry because her tears scalded her raw, red flesh.

"Hon, is this another one of your exaggerations? I know you've been complaining about sensitive skin, but I really doubt this is something most people would call a crisis."

If she'd had any hair left on the back of her neck, it would have bristled then. He was referring to her generalized anxiety disorder, which had in the past caused her to focus on small annoyances and worry excessively about everything. But this was the first time he'd used it against her. And it was when she needed his support the most.

Her mouth was too sore to waste effort on a reply. Next, she called her doctor. She got smart and used the voice command to call to save herself the pain of dialing with her fingers.

When the receptionist picked up, Helena launched into a panicked explanation of her predicament.

"I really don't think that's funny,"

Helena was afraid to be hung up on again, so she tried to make herself sound less hysterical.

"You're right. Let's schedule just a checkup, then."

With her checkup scheduled for that afternoon, she waited in a painful purgatory, trying to move her exposed limbs as little as possible. Her boyfriend hadn't called to check on her after their frosty exchange. It appeared no apology was imminent. But that was only a secondary concern. She had to get skin again, and to do that, she had to get someone to believe her.

Helena had a shirt and a skirt on to go to the doctor's office, even though the touch of the fabric burned her. The touch of everything burned her.

At reception, nobody gave her a second look. Despite Helena being able to see her grotesque reflection in the glass of a picture frame, despite the fact that her touch on the sign-in sheet left a trail of fluids, nobody seemed to notice anything unusual about her at all. Or if they did, they didn't let on. The only time she earned eye contact was when the receptionist flicked her eyes from Helena to the hand sanitizer, as if to say she expected her to use it, even in Helena's skinless condition. Never one to cause trouble, Helena did. The sanitizer burned her hands like acid, and she bit her tongue to keep from crying out.

Finally, Helena got what she wanted when she saw the doctor. He was the first person to confirm what she knew to be true: she was missing her skin.

"However," he said, shaking his head. "The treatment for this is not covered by your insurance."

"Well," Helena replied hoarsely, "how much is the out-of-pocket cost?"

He named a number that was more than she would make in 20 years at her waitressing job, a position she doubted she'd be able to keep now.

But what did it matter? She had no skin. It was an emergency. She could take out loans. Whatever was required, she would pay.

"I'll pay. I'll do anything," she croaked.

But the doctor shook his head. "I'm sorry, sweetheart. Even if you wanted to pay out of pocket, I'm afraid the surgeons wouldn't treat you. This condition is congenital. I don't believe for a minute that it happened overnight as you've claimed. I do believe that *you* believe that story. My diagnosis is that you're having an increase in your anxiety symptoms."

Helena's jaw hinged open, mouth red and gaping.

"You've survived your whole life with this congenital condition, so today is no different, is it? You'll be fine. I'm going to increase your anxiety medication by 25 milligrams, though." The doctor beamed, waiting for his thanks. "So, you'll feel much better soon, dear."

His hand gripped her shoulder as he attempted to reassure her. She cried out in pain at the touch.

As he finished typing the new information into her chart, he gave her a sidelong look and a parting piece of advice.

"Sweetie, this really could have waited, you know. I see patients with real emergencies every day. Perhaps you can consider that next time you request a same-day appointment."

And it was that comment that spurred Helena to reject the idea of ever getting help. She left everything she knew, including her boyfriend and her apartment. None of the old places in her life fit her now. But she did find a form of help, hard-won and secretive though it was, in the community of other skinless women. They formed a commune, living feral and skinless with their bared teeth. They shared the secrets of living without skin. It didn't cure, but it made things more bearable. You can find them by following the sounds of their pain echoing through the city streets.

11

Velveterror Rabbit

Lina stopped short at the riverbank, yanking Harvey back.

"Harv, it's time to go back, treasure or not. My mom's gonna' freak if I get any more camp demerits."

The last fingers of sunlight ran through the thick sweep of green trees.

"But I just *know* something good is going to be on that island. Nobody will care if we're a little late."

"Counselor Alvarez *always* cares when we're late."

Lina squatted on the sand bar and scooped up a smooth stone. "Let's just bring this rock back for the assignment. It kind of looks like a heart. It could be a treasure. Boom. Assignment complete."

"You do what you want," Harvey said, her eyes locked on the little island beyond the thin strip of water. "I'm going over there. This is the last week of camp. Who knows if I'll get another chance to come back here again?"

"Are you really not coming back next year?"

"Mom said that this camp isn't very...*value added*. She wants to send me to some STEAM camp next summer. Apparently, it would look better on my college applications."

Lina shifted on her feet before turning a withering scowl on Harvey.

"You know what counselor Alvarez always says. Never leave your camp buddy."

"*I'm* not the one leaving my buddy," Harvey said. She yanked off her sneakers and set them neatly on a large, flat rock. "You are the one splitting us up since you decided not to come with me."

"That's not how this works, and you know it."

Harvey peeled off her socks.

"We're supposed to wear life vests any time we go in water," Lina said.

"It's only a few yards. And we're both on the swim team—what are you so worried about?" Harvey plunged her feet into the river. The water was surprisingly cold, and it made her toes tingle.

"It's getting dark."

Lina stepped back, putting distance between herself and the water. "We didn't bring a flashlight."

Lina's feet stood solidly in the grass beneath the shadows of the trees.

Harvey was up to her knees in water. She shrugged.

"It's okay, Lina. You don't have to wait for me. Go back to camp. Tell counselor Alvarez I refused to go with you. I don't care. Because I'll be back before anybody notices I'm missing. You're making a big deal out of nothing."

Lina groaned, seeming to struggle with the choice. Finally, she removed the green handkerchief from her neck and tied it around a low branch in a nearby tree.

"I made a marker for you. In case you need help finding the trail when you come back."

Harvey didn't reply. Her eyes were on the islet.

The cold water made goose pimples rise on Harvey's arms and legs as she forced herself through the river.

She emerged on the pebbly shore and pulled her long hair over her shoulder. She wrung it out, unleashing a cascade of water on the rocks. She frowned at the dark brown color of her strands, remembering the stink of the hair dye when her mom had forced Harvey to dye her hair after she had returned from a slumber party with pink streaks.

"How could you do something so irresponsible when you know that you're job shadowing next week," her mother had chided her as she'd slopped the stinky chemicals over Harvey's hair. "This makes you look cheap. First impressions matter, Harvey Dell."

Harvey leaned over her knees and caught her breath. Shivering, she looked over her shoulder and considered going back. Even though her eyes were adjusting to the dark, it felt scarier now that she couldn't hold Lina's hand.

She stood. She was going to find the best treasure the camp counselor had ever seen.

She'd find something much more exciting than a stupid rock. Besides, she'd already get a demerit at this point. She at least had to make it worth something.

She stumbled through the darkness until she caught sight of faintly gleaming, beady eyes shining out from the crook of a tree. A dark lump nestled in the branches, just out of reach.

She jumped up, grabbed a branch, and swung her legs freely over the ground. After a few swings, she gained the momentum to hoist her right leg over a branch. She scooted toward the middle of the tree.

She grabbed the thing and felt its soft, velvety texture. She turned it around and examined its long, flat appendages. In the dark, she made out the profile of a stuffed rabbit.

Hello, Harvey.

The rabbit slipped from her fingers into the leaves below. Clutching the tree trunk, Harvey lowered herself to the ground. Even though her damp skin had warmed in the summer evening air, she shivered.

She picked the rabbit back up and stroked its smooth body. Both of its gleaming, black eyes seemed to watch her. Its little pink nose was so perfect that she almost imagined it wiggling. It even had thin little black stitches to delineate its mouth and the toes on its brown paws.

There wasn't any sign of mold or rot. It didn't smell of the moss and dirt of the forest. It smelled fresh off the conveyor belt of a factory.

This was a very special treasure indeed.

As Harvey turned the rabbit over in her hands, she decided not to take it back to camp. This rabbit was too special to share. The other kids wouldn't understand. And besides, she didn't know how she would get it over the river without getting it soggy and ruined. She couldn't bear the thought of that.

She found a hollow knot in the tree and placed the rabbit inside. Then she stacked a thin layer of leaves on top, protecting it from prying eyes.

"There," Harvey said as she tucked the last of the leaves inside the hole. "Now you'll be safe. I'll come back for you tomorrow. What can I call you, by the way?"

Just call me Rabbit. Come back for me tomorrow, Harvey.

Harvey felt a thrill of excitement as the words echoed in her mind.

***

As punishment for being late to return, Harvey got stuck with breakfast duty the next morning.

"Is it okay if you handle the biscuits?" Counselor Alvarez asked as she held the basket of food.

"I'm not allergic to gluten," Harvey said. She clenched her jaw. Her mom always made sure to tell the grownups everywhere that Harvey couldn't have gluten, even though she didn't have an allergy. Mom insisted all the same that the stuff was *poison* and that most carbs just were *empty calories* anyway.

"Good." Counselor Alvarez handed Harvey the load of biscuits and indicated the benches where paper plates had been laid out for breakfast.

"One for each plate, and then you can come over and help me with the eggs."

Thoughts of Rabbit and his twinkling black eyes entertained Harvey through the dull tasks. She would tell him all about this when she saw him next.

She spent the rest of breakfast plotting her next visit to Rabbit's island.

****

During the morning group hike, Harvey waited for a chance to sneak away.

As counselor Alvarez droned on about mushroom gills, colors, and texture, Harvey tuned her ear to Rabbit's whispers. She wasn't sure how she heard him—he must have been miles away by now. But his voice indeed spoke to her, as clearly as if his soft, sewn mouth murmured right next to her ear.

Come back, Harvey. Come back. I've something to show you.

Luckily for Harvey, she was sitting in the back, and Counselor Alvarez always liked to end their nature lessons with a meditation. While Counselor Alvarez and the other girls closed their eyes and listened to the sounds of squirrels and wind, Harvey slipped away.

Still, Counselor Alvarez had keen ears. Her eyes popped open, landing on Harvey with her eyebrows raised.

"Bathroom," Harvey whispered, and Counselor Alvarez nodded and closed her eyes again.

Harvey went past the curve of the trail, walking until she was out of sight. Then she ran as fast as she could, following the sound of Rabbit's whispers.

This way, Harvey.

Harvey huffed and puffed as she tore through the undergrowth. She knew she wouldn't have much time before Counselor Alvarez would start searching for her. The whole camp would be looking before long. She didn't have a plan for that part. All she knew was that she had to get to Rabbit.

Almost there, Harvey.

Finally, Harvey arrived at the riverbank. Rabbit Island waited on the other side. Dull echoes bounced off the trees: there were shouts of her name that were not from Rabbit, but rather from Counselor Alvarez and the other Tree Frog scouts. She ignored their cries and plunged into the water.

She emerged onto Rabbit Island and ran to Rabbit's tree. Her heart pounded. The yelling voices grew louder. Her pursuers were close.

She rifled through the leaves in the hollow until she found Rabbit.

Dogs barked in the near distance. Bellowing shouts from grown men rumbled through the trees behind her. Had Counselor Alvarez called the police? How long had she been running? She looked up at the sky and saw that it was afternoon. Somehow, she'd been running for hours and hadn't even noticed the time passing.

"Rabbit," she whispered, "I'm going to get in so much trouble. Can you help me?"

You'll be safe under the rock, Harvey.

Harvey ran over to a craggy outcropping. She ducked underneath the overhang, gripping Rabbit in one hand.

A splash resounded from the river. A hound bayed.

Into the hole. Behind you.

Harvey hesitated. The hole before her was pitch black, but the footsteps tromping all over Rabbit Island made her heart pound.

It's safe there, Harvey. Grownups can't go into my rabbit den.

"What about dogs?" she whispered.

Especially not dogs.

Harvey tucked Rabbit under her arm and got on her hands and knees.

It's only dark at first. Keep going a few feet, and you'll see the most beautiful lights.

Harvey felt the brush of a dog's nose just as she scooted inside.

As soon as she fully entered Rabbit's den, the exit was swallowed by darkness. Just as Rabbit had promised, the dog didn't follow. The voices that had called her were now silent.

See, Harvey? I told you it would be safe.

"Rabbit, I can't see anything. I'm so scared."

Keep going, Harvey. There's light ahead.

Harvey crawled forward, despite feeling like she might have made a mistake. Her knees and hands ached from bearing her weight through the narrow tunnel. Sharp rocks jabbed and scraped her skin.

But soon enough, just as Rabbit said, Harvey saw a silvery blue glow bounce off the earthen walls ahead. She crawled faster, eager to get out of the suffocating dark. She turned a corner, and the tunnel opened into a wide, expansive cave.

Brilliant, iridescent stars studded the roof of the massive cave. Harvey marveled at the beauty of the cool, white light shining down.

"Stars? But it's the middle of the day!"

Not here. This is a new world. A world that only very special children get to see.

Harvey spread her arms wide and twirled under the winking lights. The beautiful dance of light and shadow made her fears dissolve.

"It's beautiful, Rabbit!"

Wait until you see what's next. Keep going, Harvey.

A trickle of pale pink light streamed in from an opening at the other end of the cave. Harvey emerged from the cave, blinking her eyes in the intense light. As her vision adjusted, the world opened into a landscape unlike anything she'd ever seen.

The mouth of the cave yawned open from the base of a great mountain. Harvey shivered in the cold wind with her tennis shoes plunged deep into a snowbank. A few yards ahead, a large body of liquid formed a giant lake. Amazingly, there was no ice covering it.

The lake seemed alive, swirling with red and white patterns, reminding Harvey of melted candy canes. Overhead, the sky blushed bright pink instead of blue. It was not the ombré pink of a sunset—the entire sky was solid pink from top to horizon.

"What is this place? It's beautiful."

It's a magical place. A place of dreams, Harvey.

"I didn't bring a coat. It's so cold."

It won't be long before we get where we're going. It's warm there.

Harvey bit her trembling lip, feeling a tingle of unease at the base of her neck.

"I want to go back and get a coat. I'll come back later."

Harvey turned back toward the cave and followed her footsteps back through the snow.

Wait!

Harvey paused.

If you go back, the grownups will be so mad. They will never let you go anywhere again.

Harvey weighed her options. No matter what, the grownups would be upset. What did she have to lose by exploring a little before returning?

And if you leave, you can't come back here again, Harvey. The cave only lets you in once.

"It's not much farther?"

It's so close, Harvey.

"Okay."

Rabbit guided Harvey to a little boat on the edge of the candy cane lake. It was made of old, gnarled wood, and Harvey feared that it wouldn't make it across.

But she had already made her decision.

She climbed into the rickety boat and pushed off the snowy shore using one of the oars. Her arms ached as she rowed toward their next destination—an island in the middle of the swirling lake.

An island within an island.

When a red, glowing fish leaped out of the water, Harvey almost dropped one of the oars.

"What is that?" she exclaimed.

A gumdrop fish. They taste delicious.

As Harvey rowed to the shore of the small island, dozens of gumdrop fish flanked their boat, leaping in all directions. The sight of it made her laugh despite the frigid cold.

Harvey was still wearing her shorts from camp, and melted snow soaked through her sneakers as she stepped onto shore. Lethargy overtook her, and she wanted to turn the boat over and huddle under it for warmth.

Keep going, Harvey!

Pine trees flanked a small path in the snow. A set of small human footprints lead the way before her path.

"Did someone else come here today, Rabbit?"

Oh yes. I have many friends, and they all like to bring their favorite children here.

The pine trees opened into a clearing full of old-fashioned toys. There were rocking horses, jack-in-the-boxes, teddy bears, dolls, tin soldiers, and more, all sitting in a circle in the clearing. There must have been hundreds of them. The other child's footsteps stopped at a doll with red yarn for hair. Harvey didn't see signs of that kid anywhere.

Normally, Harvey would be excited to see this many toys, but something seemed wrong about them in such a place all alone, in such a formation.

"Is this what you wanted me to see?"

Almost. Sit, Harvey.

Harvey sat in the cold snow. Her face, fingers, and toes were numb. She remembered the Tree Frog scout lesson on frostbite, and she worried that this was the start of it.

Now, set me down next to you and say, "Rabbit, I wish you were real."

The thought of a pet rabbit thrilled Harvey, even in her cold-induced stupor. Her frigid, blue lips formed the words as she was asked.

"Rabbit, I wish you were real," she whispered.

Immediately, Harvey's perspective toppled several feet lower to the ground. She turned her head, which felt stiff and soft at the same time, and she saw her own body sitting next to her.

Harvey looked down at her arms and legs. They weren't her own limbs—they were the velvety smooth haunches and paws that belonged to Rabbit. She tried to scream, but no sound came out from the few thin lines of stitched black thread. Her new mouth wiggled like a worm, soundless and useless. She tried to stand and couldn't.

Rabbit, wearing Harvey's body, ran away from her without saying another word.

Harvey pleaded with her thoughts, trying to speak to Rabbit like he had spoken with her before, but it was no use. She watched Rabbit take her body back into the boat and row away. She heard the splashes of the gumdrop fish as Rabbit rowed out of sight.

Rabbit had been right. In this stuffed animal's body, she wasn't cold. She couldn't feel anything at all. She couldn't even cry.

***

Rabbit had to hurry before Harvey's body succumbed to the cold. There were so many times that Rabbit had tread this path, but this was the first time that he had ever succeeded in getting a child to take his place.

It had been such a long time that Rabbit didn't remember who he had been before *he* had become Rabbit so many years ago.

But Rabbit focused on the positives. For example, the farther away he got from the island, the less he would hear Harvey screaming in his mind.

And, as far as Harvey's family was concerned, Rabbit would bring Harvey back to them. Rabbit would make Harvey the best daughter that they could imagine. Rabbit would do everything they asked without complaint because Rabbit was finally *real* again. Being real again was all Rabbit had ever wanted during his lonely years on the island.

Rabbit stood on the edge of the forest. He undid the knot of a green handkerchief that had been tied around a low-hanging branch.

With hands that still had Harvey's muscle memory, he tied the handkerchief in a bow around Harvey's ponytail.

And if Harvey didn't like her new life on the island? Well, she knew the way out, and the world was full of children who could take her place.

12

The Safe Test

Yesterday they'd fought about the safe again. But today they pretended everything was fine.

Carina touched Luke's shoulder as he passed on his way out the door. "I'm going to miss you," she said. But wasn't there a rush of anticipation? Didn't her toes wiggle in her shoes as if they couldn't wait to tiptoe into the bedroom and discover what he'd been hiding from her?

"It's always hard to be apart," he replied, leaning in close. The sharp woody notes of his aftershave met her nostrils. His lips grazed her forehead as he said, "I hope you do okay for the next few days."

Carina drew her long cable-knit sweater closer and looked up into his brown eyes. "I'll be fine. Don't worry."

"Good luck, sweetheart," he said as he ruffled her short chestnut hair. She jerked away and smoothed it down.

"Right," Carina said. "Good luck to you too. I hope you make the sale."

She hadn't told him that she'd taken the next three days off from her work at the publishing house and was ready to tackle that safe while he was gone. The way she saw it, since they were living together, she deserved to know what was in that safe.

After Luke left, she watched bad daytime television for about an hour, just in case he forgot something and decided to come back and surprise her in the act. When she was reasonably certain that she was alone, she locked the front door and prepared herself.

It was simple. She'd find a way to open the safe, even if it took a call to a locksmith or the safe manufacturer. Once she knew what was inside, she was sure that her nagging feelings of distrust would leave her.

In the past, whenever she'd tried to explain to him why the secrecy bothered her, he'd gotten defensive. After that, she'd coped by bringing it up in a joking manner, referring to heads and fingers that he might have stashed there in his secret second life as a serial killer. But after a few months, the joking had turned to fervent pleading and threats to leave him if he didn't share what was inside the safe.

In the best-case scenario, it was something so banal that it would be laughable that he was embarrassed to show it to her. Something like his old high-school yearbook photos or the amateur records he once made in a garage band. In the worst case—well, she hadn't considered the worst case. And she didn't think she needed to.

She walked to the small galley kitchen and pulled her sleeves down over her hands. As she cradled a cup of dark-roast coffee and felt the warmth enter her hands, a sense of calm also flowed through her. She took long, slow sips, watching the steam rise into the air until it was finished.

In the bedroom, they'd left the white sheets crumpled on the bed and clothes were strewn about on the floor. She stepped over the clothes and made her way to the closet.

The safe was there like always. She'd almost expected Luke to take it with him on his trip. He seemed paranoid enough to. For a moment, she thought about letting it be. By leaving her alone with the safe, he'd shown her a small bit of trust. Perhaps she shouldn't break it. Maybe if she could be patient and continue to show him that she was trustworthy, he'd eventually tell her what he'd been hiding.

Nah.

Carina was ashamed to admit it, but she enjoyed the feeling of goosebumps on her forearms at the thought of sneaking behind his back. There was something thrilling about a break-in. It simply wouldn't be as fun if he gave up his secrets willingly.

There weren't any heating vents in the dark closet, and Carina shivered despite her sturdy cable-knit sweater. Freezing cold metal met her fingers as she stroked the safe. It was black and smooth and blank, except for a keypad and small silver handle. Her fingers bumped into the edge of something on top of the safe. It was a picture of something but she couldn't see clearly in the dark closet.

She emerged from the tiny room and went over to the bed to look at the picture. It was an art print with a familiar tableau: a funny little old man, a girl with golden hair, and a spinning wheel transforming straw to gold. *Rumpelstiltskin,* Carina thought.

It was strange to see it here, considering that she'd never known Luke to be a fan of anything impractical, let along art or fairy tales. It had to mean something, but whether it had anything to do with the contents of the safe she couldn't be sure. Was Luke hiding a secret stash of gold inside? Did he consider himself someone who turns common things into money? She guessed that was technically what salespeople did. Maybe he just found the print inspirational somehow.

She had three days while Luke would be gone. There was no rush. So, she decided to go blindly guessing about at the safe combination using his birthday and favorite numbers. It would be almost a little disappointing if that strategy worked, but at least she'd get to feel a little superior. But when she put the picture face-down on the bed, something else caught her eye. There were strange, deliberate markings on the back of the frame.

It didn't take her long to realize that they were blanks. Word blanks.

Faced with this new development, Carina laid back on the bed and gazed past the ceiling. It was a hint. But why? Luke had been so stubborn about making sure she never opened the safe, but here he'd left her a clue for how to do that very thing.

Now she was even more determined than ever. It seemed like he *wanted* her to open the safe. Otherwise, why would he have left these clues? It was an outright dare.

She set to work immediately, trying to think of what the blanks had to do with her, with Luke, with the safe, or with the picture. She snatched a notebook from her nightstand and a pencil.

There were 15 blanks. It didn't take long for her to realize that the main character depicted in the picture also had 15 letters in his name: *Rumpelstiltskin.*

"It's an anagram!" she exclaimed out loud with a little laugh. It seemed increasingly likely that she was being guided toward a specific end. This was a test that had been designed just for her, surely. And she was going to solve it and show Luke just how smart she was.

She started out with high spirits, but by noon her eyelids began to feel heavy as she scanned the pages of nonsense she'd made by combining various letters from *Rumpelstiltskin.* A wreath of chicken-scratch surrounded her on the papers. She stood up and stretched, thinking that it was about time for a nap to refresh herself. But with the change in perspective, her eyes caught upon a combination that she hadn't thought of before.

L's trumpet is link

It was possible that the words were nonsense. It could be that it was her own wishful thinking making sense out of something that wasn't actually an anagram at all. However, Luke did sign all his letters as *L* and he did own a trumpet, so Carina decided to follow the path.

The trumpet was on a stand in the living room. She found it unlikely that there was a note tucked inside the opening that had evaded her notice, but she peered down the mouth and the end of the instrument anyway. Empty as always. She blew into it just to be sure nothing would come flying out. It didn't.

She made a half-hearted attempted at playing a sputtering note to express her disappointment before putting it back on the stand. She sat on the couch and pressed her forehead into her hands.

What was she thinking? This was absurd. She wasn't in a detective novel. People didn't just leave scrambled hints around for their significant others to find. She should just go have a spa day like a normal girlfriend without trust issues.

But right as she was about to get dressed to go out, a silver sparkle drew her back in. She watched the clasp of the trumpet case glint in the light. She stood and grabbed the case from its spot on the floor, desperately, as if her self-respect depended on it.

She turned it over in her hands and opened the clasps to reveal the blue velvet inside. On the top of the lid, where the brand name was displayed, there was a model number.

Gasping, she took the case over to the closet.

She copied the model number into the keypad but the safe didn't open. Beads of sweat slid down her temples despite the cold. Perhaps she'd just put the number in wrong. Her fingers, she suddenly noticed, were shaking. She shook her hands to loosen them before trying again.

A beep sounded, and then a click as the lock disengaged. Carina whooped, sighed, and then rocked back to sit on her heels, staring at the safe.

She'd finally done it.

Now she felt terrified. Somehow, she knew that if she looked into the safe nothing would ever be the same in their relationship. As soon as the lock had disengaged, she felt that whatever was inside this box wasn't something merely embarrassing or trivial. She felt, deep down in her core, that she was getting closer and closer to something extremely dangerous.

But that only made her want to open it more. Now the thing was close. Whatever had been keeping her from trusting Luke fully was right at her fingertips. She could almost feel waves of energy coming from it, beckoning her to see.

She closed her eyes, bit her lip, and shook her head. Then, she opened the door.

It was empty.

Carina wiped her forehead. An empty safe? All the time, all this paranoia, and it had been empty?

She reached her hand in and felt a small rectangular object taped to the roof of the safe. She yanked and pulled at it until it came free.

A flash drive lay in her palm. It was black, and unlabeled, and very, very cold.

There was no more hesitation left in Carina, only a relentless drive to *know*. She dashed to her laptop and connected the flash drive.

Pictures and videos flashed before her eyes, overtaking the entire landscape of the screen. At first, Carina thought she'd stumbled upon a random porn collection. But then she began to recognize Luke in the videos. There were dozens of other women with him. You could see their faces. Carina covered her mouth with both of her hands and groaned. Frantic, she pressed *Esc*, and then *CRTL + ALT + DELETE*, but nothing would rid the screen of the deluge of video content. Each video sprang up in a separate window like a popup ad and would not close even if she pressed the red X. They littered her screen like a scattered deck of cards.

But then, the worst thing of all happened—she recognized her own face in a video. She screamed and threw the laptop to the floor, racing out of the room. She braced herself against the wall, holding her arms around her body and letting tears stream down her face.

Then, she heard Luke's voice coming from her laptop's speakers.

"You just couldn't leave it alone, could you?" Luke said.

Carina stumbled back into the room and picked the laptop up, feeling like she was in a dream.

"I've been waiting for a woman I can trust. If you're listening to this message, then you're not it. The safe was a test and you failed."

"You have three days to get me $500,000. Consider this our breakup, and you'll give me a nice little parting gift to apologize for your treachery. And if you don't get me this money in time, all your email contacts will receive your little sex-tape debut. Don't bother destroying the flash drive. It's already grabbed control of your pc and it has access to your email accounts."

Three days, Carina mouthed. It was down to money now. Their entire year-long relationship, now reduced to a contract. No, not a contract—blackmail.

"And before you think about involving the police, here's something else: you don't even know my real name. I go by a lot of names." Here, he laughed and smirked at the camera, as if encouraging the viewer to consider how charming and clever he was.

Suddenly, the video windows all closed, including the one with the message from Luke. All that was left was the flash drive folder. She looked at the file inside: Pandora.exe. She clicked it.

There was a button that appeared that simply said *Transfer funds now*. A text file appeared with detailed instructions for transferring funds into cryptocurrency. He wanted her to load all the money onto a flash drive and mail it to a P.O. box.

She moaned and laid her head on the keyboard. So this was what she had fought so hard to reveal: her own ruin. On the other hand, she was appalled to realize that she had been living with this criminal for a whole year. She banged her head on the keys a few times for good measure.

She thought again of the picture on his safe: Luke had seen her as the worthless straw he'd been spinning into future wealth. She and all those other women he'd videotaped.

Perhaps there was still a chance to salvage things. Maybe she could take out the flash drive, get her computer treated for malware, and then replace everything in the safe just like it was. Maybe Luke would never know she'd opened it as long as she could keep the secret. Then she could pick up one night and leave without a trace, or find an excuse to break up, before he had a chance to blackmail her.

But of course, Luke's program had already closed that possibility. She saw a new email notification and read the message with dread. Just two words from Luke in the subject with nothing in the body of the message: *I know.* The program on the flash drive must have notified him as soon as it began running. There was no way out now. Unless...

Carina had three days to get him his money. Or three days to guess his real name, and find out who Luke really was, and make him pay.

A ring at the door pulled her out of her thoughts. The video doorbell showed Luke's face at the door, clothed in a black jacket with the hood up, with a harrowing smile. And the only thing keeping him from coming inside was the chain on the inside.

It was then that Carina realized that there had never been a business trip, and that Luke had never actually left town. This whole thing was a trap he'd planned, and she'd been caught completely unaware. Now he was here to ensure that she paid the money, if the video threats hadn't been enough.

Carina screamed as Luke slipped a knife through the crack in the door, sliding the chain off in one fluid stroke.

13

❧

Preview: The Haunting of Watermill Valley

The following is an excerpt from K.M. Bennett's upcoming novel, The Haunting of Watermill Valley, set to release in early 2025.

Of course the moving truck crashed. Nothing about this move had gone smoothly. Amelia Ruiz had come to expect things to be a disaster as a matter of course. Thankfully, her friend Noah lived in this town and was able to pick her up from where she'd been stranded on the median after her wreck. As they rolled down the suburban streets in his like-new blue Toyota Corolla, she tried to dodge his questions about how life had been since they'd last known each other in college. She'd gathered that he was doing pretty well for himself and was moving up the ladder as an investment banker.

But Amelia had little to show since her college days except for a string of failed relationships, frequent job changes, and decisions that generally hadn't panned out. She was dreading the part where they would pull up into the driveway and he'd see the humble two-bedroom house that would have been such an upgrade for her and Erik. She could tell by the gleam of Noah's new shoes and his casual but well-made cardigan that his house that he shared with their mutual friend Gianna had at least four bedrooms, a pool, and rolling fields of tidy grass that were no doubt maintained by someone else.

"Are you sure you don't need some help getting set up here? Gianna and I don't mind, especially with you on your own. We can bring the kids with their iPads and they won't be any trouble."

Amelia smiled at her friend and tugged on the handle of her tote bag from the backseat. The bag was a sun-faded red with a black apple pattern. The scent of better days wafted from its fibers: sun, sand, and campfires. The bag and its contents were the only things she'd been able to save from the road. She squeezed it to her chest for a moment and breathed in the sweet, musky odor.

"No. You already helped so much. I just needed a ride to my place. In some ways, moving is easier now with less furniture!" She smiled even as she felt her chest tighten. The image of her few pieces of meager furniture strewn across the highway in pieces still made her feel depressed. But she had to maintain a positive attitude. If she fell into the well of depression, she didn't think she'd be able to claw her way out this time.

She supposed she should feel lucky. A scratch above her ear alerted her to a stray piece of glass that had become lodged in her dark wavy hair. The pieces of glass seemed never-ending. Just like her problems. It was starting to seem like she would just keep finding sharp slices of trouble anywhere she turned in life, in dark corners and places where she least expected it.

But she couldn't manage to carry on with that kind of attitude, so she had to start believing that things would get better. Call it kismet, karma, or faith. Call it poetic justice. But Amelia felt that the universe owed her some good luck after all she'd been through.

Buzz. Buzz. Buzz.

She pressed *ignore* on her phone below her ex's face. She had nothing to say to the guy who had convinced her to take out a solo loan for this house. The guy who ditched her the night before the move because he'd accidentally fallen in love with someone else. The guy who had convinced her to buy a house in a town where she knew nobody because he wanted the location near the motocross track. Yeah, that guy could go fuck himself.

"If you say so. But I wish you'd let us help." Noah's eyes were knit with concern. It seemed that becoming a parent had sharpened his bullshit sensors. "Are you going to have another vehicle soon?"

"Yeah," she said, confident this time. "Thankfully my insurance proved to be more reliable than my ex."

Noah laughed but the unease lingered in his eyes.

"I get to pick up a rental tomorrow," She assured him as she eyed the little white house with black shingles. There was one shingle missing right in the middle. Another on the right side was trembling in the wind, looking just as jittery as she felt inside.

"Okay. Gianna has the afternoon off, so just give her a call when you need a ride to pick it up."

"Thank you both so much," she said as tears pricked the back of her eyes. She put her arm out and gave Noah a heartfelt hug. "I really can't tell you how screwed I would have been if you hadn't come out after the wreck. You're the only people I know here."

"Don't mention it," Noah said. As he pulled away from the hug, his eyes narrowed as he looked at the property. "That's funny," he said. He pointed at the stone lions that flanked the driveway.

"Yeah, it is a little pretentious to have stone lions in front of such a tiny house." Her face flushed with embarrassment.

"Oh no," Noah quickly corrected. "That's not it. It's just that they're facing the house. Normally they are turned toward the outside. Kind of like they are protecting the place." He popped a piece of gum into his mouth and the smell of spearmint filled the air. "These are watching the house instead," he said.

Amelia accepted the stick of gum he offered.

The stone statues were watching the house. Why was it that she hadn't noticed that before? As she took the lions in, in with their gaping maws and scowling eyes, a trickle of ice entered her veins.

"Guess the previous owners wanted to be able to wake up to the view of those beautiful smiling faces," she quipped.

She made a mental note that if she stayed in this house for long, she'd find a way to tear those creepy statues down. After Noah drove off and she approached the screen door, she felt the sensation of eyes following her as she passed.

***

Amelia didn't have a lot of clothes to spare, considering many of them had been ruined when they'd all spilled over the highway during the wreck. But she had to do something about the lions. All that first night in the new house she'd been unable to sleep because of them. It didn't make any sense but somehow, she could *feel* them staring at the house.

No, not at the house. At *her*.

She had never been one to buy into ideas about energy or auras or spirits, and yet she found herself without explanation for the sensations brought on by the statues. The word she settled on was *presence*. They had a presence to them, and it was terrifying the living daylights out of her.

So that's how she found herself outside at six a.m. after a sleepless night, wearing her faded men's boxer briefs and a ratty old Led Zeppelin tee. A small bundle of clothes in her hand, she padded toward the lions. When a stray rock found its way right under her foot, she yelped. As she wrapped a pink bandana around the rightmost lion's neck, she saw her next-door neighbor walk to their car. In the dark she saw the outline of a middle-aged woman with curly hair and a pantsuit. They locked eyes and she felt her stomach drop with embarrassment at being caught dressing her lions in her flimsy pajamas.

"Hi," Amelia waved. She put on a smile despite her embarrassment.

Although the woman had seemed to lock eyes with Amelia in the meager morning light, she either hadn't noticed her or *pretended* not to have seen or heard her. She turned her head away and climbed into her car. When the woman drove away, Amelia tried again to wave to no effect.

"Okay," she breathed. She felt shaky again. She finished dressing the lion on the left with a scarf. The final touch on each was a pink ribbon wrapped into a neat bow on the end of their tails.

"Not so scary now, are you?" She said. Surveying her work with her hands on her hips, she smiled despite the feeling that she had barely dented the foreboding wall of repulsion that surrounded the lions. They stared back at her, impassive, but only in the way the Queen of England's guards could be described as *impassive*. Just because they were still and frozen like statues didn't mean they weren't alive behind their watchful eyes, waiting for the right moment to strike.

She laughed at herself. Where was she getting these silly thoughts? It was obviously just a fixation that her mind had chosen as a distraction from the stress. A breakup, a car crash, a solo surprise mortgage that she'd thought her ex's income would be contributing to. These lions must have reminded her of the macho impulse to make everything as big and imposing as possible to make up for the fact that there was a bunch of nothing inside. No wonder she wanted to take a sledgehammer to them.

She doubted she could make enough money to hire any but the most dubious contractors on a server's wages, but she still told herself that she would ask Gianna if she had any recommendations for someone to destroy those lions.

Turning her back on them, she went back into the house and managed to take a nap until ten a.m. She had the sensation upon waking that she'd had a bad dream, due to the fact that a slick film of sweat covered her entire body and her heart was pounding. But when she tried to think of what had caused such a response in her, it was like tuning in to static.

When the alarm went off shortly after she awoke like this, she smacked the off button and groaned. It was already time to dress and get ready for Gianna to take her to the car rental, and she felt like she hadn't slept at all.

The morning was quiet as she unpacked her tote bag of belongings. She had a protein bar and a glass of tap water at the blue Formica countertop in the kitchen. It was a nice place, even though it felt like it came from another century. It needed some love, that was true. But every apartment she'd ever lived in had needed work. Her eyes roamed the peeling edges of rabbit-print wallpaper in the north corner of the kitchen.

For the first time, she felt an expansiveness in her chest at the idea of living alone. All her life, she'd lived either with her parents, a room-mate, or her ex. She hadn't been thrilled to be saddled with a mortgage on her own, but in the quiet dawn light of her little galley kitchen, she found herself imagining the possibilities. She could go for a cot-tage core look here. It was the perfect size for it. And the only person she'd have to answer to was herself. Herself and her meager budget, that was. There was something freeing in being on your own. Maybe it didn't have to be terrifying at all. Maybe it could be an adventure.

Still, it sucked that her ex had left her like this. It would have been better if she'd planned this particular adventure.

She took off her clothes and headed for the shower, shivering as she sensed that those lions were somehow still watching through the walls. After stepping over the lip of the bathtub, her foot was immersed in a wet, gelatinous puddle that squelched and spread into the spaces be-tween her toes. Touching the cold substance was so shocking that she yanked her foot back and twisted her ankle, plummeting backward toward the yellowed linoleum.

Acknowledgements

First, I would like to thank you, the reader, for being here and giving me so much of your time and attention. In a world where so many things are vying for your eyeballs, it is no small thing that you have taken the time to read my work. Thank you so much.

Thank you to the people who have read some of these stories in the draft stages: Dakota Bennett, Nicole Edens, and Jess. I always appreciate your insights, and your support has meant the world to me.

Thanks to my friends who make this journey fun. All work and no play makes Jack a dull boy, after all. Thanks, Julie Brooks and Rachel D., for being steadfast friends for many years. Love to the Callaway family as well.

Thanks to Jessica for being my horror mom-friend. We are unicorns in the Midwest, and I'm so glad we found each other. Thanks to her family for letting me borrow her for writing shenanigans!

Thanks to my former JHA coworkers who have always been so supportive of my fiction work. I so appreciate how you all have cheered me on.

Thank you to my HWA mentor, Rachel A. You helped give me confidence in my work. I am so grateful for your investment in me.

Thanks to my chapter of the Horror Writers Association. I love being in your group and have gotten so many benefits from it. Thanks especially to Amanda for starting it all.

Thanks to my mom and family for loving me even though I write really weird, gross stuff.

Shoutout to my husband's family, who are always so great about supporting my work.

Thanks to my dad, who always read my work with enthusiasm and once called me "the smartest girl in the world." I hope you're reading from heaven.

My husband, Dakota: you could write your own book about the care and feeding of authors. I love you. Your support is everything.

Thanks to my kids for being so cute and for being my biggest fans. I love you. Don't read this until you're much, much older.

About The Author

K.M. Bennett lives in the midwestern U.S. She has a Master of Arts in Writing, and her work has been featured in several podcasts, including the *NoSleep Podcast*, *Nighty Night with Rabia Chaudry* podcast, and *Thirteen* podcast. Her short stories have also been featured in multiple small-press anthologies.

During the day, she works as a technical editor. She lives with her husband, two kids, and two rescue dogs. She is a scaredy-cat who is still afraid of the dark.

Can't get enough horror from K.M. Bennett? Here's how to get more involved as a fan:

- Never miss a new release! Sign up for K.M. Bennett's newsletter at kmbennett.substack.com.
- Visit her Amazon Author page at amazon.com/author/kmbennett or her website, ThatKatieLady.com.
- Become a member at www.patreon.com/k.m._bennett and get behind-the-scenes posts, microfiction stories, exclusive content, and other fun surprises.
- Follow:
    - facebook.com/ThatKatieLady
    - instagram.com/k.m._bennett.
- Review! Leave reviews of this book anywhere you can, such as on Amazon or Goodreads. Every review supports the author and helps others find her work.